THE HALLOWED ÎSLE

BOOK ONE:

THE BOOK OF THE SWORD

Other Books by
Diana L. Paxson

The Serpent's Tooth
The White Raven

Wodan's Children *Trilogy*

The Dragons of the Rhine
The Wolf and the Raven
The Lord of Horses

With Adrienne Martine-Barnes

Master of Earth and Water
The Shield Between the Worlds
Sword of Fire and Shadow

THE HALLOWED ISLE

BOOK ONE:
THE BOOK OF THE SWORD

DIANA L. PAXSON

AVON · EOS

This is a work of fiction. Names, characters, places, and incidents either are the product of the author's imagination or are used fictitiously. Any resemblance to actual events, locales, organizations, or persons, living or dead, is entirely coincidental and beyond the intent of either the author or the publisher.

AVON BOOKS, INC.
1350 Avenue of the Americas
New York, New York 10019

Copyright © 1999 by Diana L. Paxson
Published by arrangement with the author
Visit our website at **http://www.AvonBooks.com/Eos**
ISBN: 0-380-78870-5

Library of Congress Cataloging in Publication Data:

Paxson, Diana L.
  The hallowed isle / by Diana L. Paxson.
    p.   cm.
  Contents: bk. 1. The book of the sword—
    1. Great Britain—History—Anglo Saxon period. 449–1066—Fiction.
2. Arthurian romances—Adaptations.   3. Arthur, King—Fiction.
I. Title.
PS3566.A897H35   98-49035
813'.54—dc21   CIP

First Avon Eos Trade Printing: February 1999

AVON EOS TRADEMARK REG. U.S. PAT. OFF. AND IN OTHER COUNTRIES, MARCA REGIS-TRADA, HECHO EN U.S.A.

Printed in the U.S.A.

OPM   10   9   8   7   6   5   4   3   2   1

In Memoriam
Paul Edwin Zimmer

ACKNOWLEDGMENTS

My special thanks to Heather Rose Jones, who took time off from her doctoral studies in Welsh philology to advise me on the mysteries of fifth-century British spelling. I would also like to thank Alexei Kondratiev for his suggestions regarding the origins of the Wild Man legend.

I direct the reader to the work of C. Scott Littleton and Ann C. Thomas for more information on the Sarmatian origins of Excalibur. For those who would like an excellent historical overview of the Arthurian period, I recommend *The Age of Arthur* by John Morris, recently reprinted by Barnes & Noble.

Through the fields of European literature, the Matter of Britain flows as a broad and noble stream. I offer this tributary with thanks and recognition to all those who have gone before.

CONTENTS

PROLOGUE

T HE FIRST LIVING THING WAS FIRE.

Erupting from the silent womb of infinite space, it devoured all matter within its reach, grew, raging, and expelled bright showers of sparks to beget new flames. Fire lives still in the glowing heart of the world and in the sun that shines above. All green and growing things feed on that light; it burns in the red blood that pulses through each vein, and in death, all become food and fuel for other things.

Fire is magic.

Above the waving grasses of the steppe, light slashes through the heavens and a solitary tree explodes into flame. Chanting, men carry away the burning branches and fire the coals in their forge. Cunning ironsmiths, their magic is composed equally of skill and spells.

Soon the hearth is ablaze, and in the trough, a lump of rock that fell from heaven begins to glow. It bubbles and cracks, flows out in a river of liquid fire to fill the mold. Once more it grows solid. Sparks fly as hammers beat out the hot iron bar into a shining wire. Again the metal is heated; glowing bundles of wire twining together, fire sparking furiously as the hammer strikes once more.

Twined and twisted, cooled and heated, each particle in each rod is realigned until the mass is no longer iron but something more. As the earth was born out of a spinning star, the steel is born from the forgefire. From the whispering of the flames grow whispered spells; each hammer stroke beats out a complex rhythm; and the steel sings in triumph as its apotheosis nears.

The mage-smiths' chanting compels the steel to hold its shape, slim and deadly and beautiful. Their spells impress upon that shape its nature and its name. They cry out to their god, drawing down his power, precise and anxious lest their work be too weak to contain what comes.

Again the bellows heave and the forge fire furiously glows. Again the blade is heated; the chant marks out the time, wise eyes watch the colors change, and now, with a cry, the steel is lifted. Its shining length seems to ripple as heat-shimmer blurs the air. The mage-smith wraps its tang in leather, and quenches the blade in the heartblood of a captive warrior, chosen for his courage on the field. Sheathed in that throbbing flesh, the sword drinks life. The blade is jerked free, and blood gushes onto the ground. The mage-smith raises it, and lightning sears the sky.

Seven smiths alone know all the spells and secrets to make these blades, the seven mages of the Chalybes. Seven swords they have crafted, forged from star-steel, bearing in their hearts the war-god's name. To seven sacred kings they are given, to deal death in the service of life.

Fire is power.

I

CEREMONY OF THE SWORD

A.D. 424—25

BRITANNIA WAS BURNING.

Artoria Argantel pulled her veil half across her face and took a careful breath, staring at the flames. She told herself that this one burning villa was not the world, but even the sun seemed afire in a molten sky, and blue smoke hazed the hills. Her cousin Maderun coughed painfully, then pulled the mantle that covered her bronze-brown hair down as if to shut out the sight of what had once been a prosperous estate. It was a smoldering ruin now, and another column of smoke beyond the hazel wood bore witness to the fate of the next farm along the road.

"Lady, you must come away—" Junius Lupercus reached for her bridle rein. The mare danced nervously as Argantel pulled her back.

"Not yet." He was only doing his duty as captain of her escort, but he did not understand why she had to see.

She stared at the bodies that lay sprawled on the trampled ground. The nearest had been an old man. Blood from a great gash in his crown stained his white hair, but he still clutched a legionary spatha and shield. *A veteran*, she thought, *who had settled near the fort he once defended*. She nudged the mare for-

3

ward. Junius reached out once more to stop her, but she was already looking at the thing he had not wanted her to see.

Behind the man a little girl, perhaps his granddaughter, stared sightlessly at the sky. The corpse of a red-haired barbarian lay across her bloodied thighs. At least the old soldier had avenged her before he himself was struck down.

"Who did this?" Maderun asked in a shaking voice, putting back her veil.

"Dalriadan raiders, come over from Hibernia," Junius said grimly, pointing at the bloodstained length of checkered cloth. "They will have landed at Bremetennacum and raided northward."

"That's where we met your ship—" said Argantel, her gaze moving from her cousin to the body of the little girl and back again. Maderun nodded, her eyes widening in comprehension.

The captain grimaced. "You were lucky, my lady. Their ships have no comforts, but they are agile and swift. The boat that brought you here would have had no chance if they had caught her at sea." He had evidently given up trying to spare them knowledge of danger.

Maderun grew, if possible, more pale, and Argantel swallowed. At that moment, her cousin's white face and gray eyes must be a mirror of her own. Barbarian raiders, whether from the Scottii or the tribes of Alba who had never come under the yoke of Rome, had been a fact of their lives for as long as they could remember. But for Argantel, learning her lessons among the priestesses of the Isle of Maidens, and for Maderun, safe in her father's court at Maridunum, the attacks had been only a tale of terror.

Until now.

"They must be punished!" she exclaimed. "They cannot be more than a half day ahead of us! Go after them, Junius!"

"And leave you undefended? I will not betray my oath to protect the Lady of the Lake, even at her command. Come, my lady, let me take you home—" He gestured northward. "There is nothing we can do here."

Home. . . . She peered through the smoke as if she could see through its filthy veils to the green mountains that rose beyond. No enemy had ever penetrated those forests and fells. Even the Romans had built no more than a guardpost there, and soon abandoned it. She closed her eyes, remembering the silver lake within its circle of sheltering heights and the tree-clad island it protected. No raider would ever breach the Isle of Maidens' sanctity. Then she looked at Junius once more and shook her head.

"These people trusted us to defend them and we failed. I will not leave them for the wild beasts to devour." Argantel straightened in the saddle, drawing about her the aura of the high priestess as she held his gaze. "Lay them in the ashes of their home and pile more wood over them. If it can no longer shelter them, let it be their pyre."

She could feel his resistance, but her will compelled him. Even Maderun, watching at her side, eyed her uneasily, as if she could see that invisible mantling of power. It would not be surprising, thought Argantel. Maderun was untrained, but their mothers had been twins, the elder bound to become Lady of the Lake and carry on the family tradition on the druid isle, the younger married off to Carmelidus, the lord of Maridunum. Argantel's hair was more red, and she was seven years older, but they looked enough alike to be sisters. She turned her awareness from the residue of fury and fear that hung like smoke in the air and fixed it on the girl.

"*Don't fear,*" she sent the thought on a wave of reassurance, "*the ones who did this are nowhere near. I would know.*" From Maderun she sensed astonishment, and then relief.

"How could this happen?" her cousin said aloud. "How could God allow it?"

Of course, thought Argantel, Maderun had been raised a Christian. But her question went beyond theology.

"God, or the gods?" she said bitterly. "Your clerics say that these disasters are a punishment for our sins. But whatever evils the old man might have done, I cannot believe that little girl deserved such agony. The god of the Christians does not protect his worshippers, and the gods of Rome fled with the legions."

"Then who will you pray to?" exclaimed Maderun. "Who will give us justice now?"

"I am sworn to serve the Lady who is the soul of this land," said Argantel slowly. "But I think the time has come to wake a different power. By oath I am a priestess of the Goddess, but by blood I have the right to call on the God in the Sword. It is dangerous, but I will dare it. You have the right as well as I, Maderun. Will you stand with me?"

Maderun gazed at the flames of the villa where the bodies of the folk who had lived there were burning. The firelight lent color to her cheeks, and glittered in the tears that filled her eyes. After a few moments she shivered and turned to Argantel again.

"I have no training in such arts as you have learned, but I hope my courage is the equal of yours. In God's name I swear that I will stand behind you, cousin, and do whatever I can to help defend our land."

Maderun reached out and Argantel took her hand. Where their flesh touched she felt a tingling, and then that odd shift in awareness that came when she directed her attention to the gods.

"May the Holy Mother bless us," she whispered, feeling Maderun's wordless assent like an echo, "and bless Britannia!"

The Sword stood upright in the altar stone. Sometimes, as a shift in the air fanned the flames of the tall torches set to either side, it would catch their light and refract a fiery flicker across the stone floor, as if something that lived within had momentarily awakened. Then it would become plain steel, a third of its length sunk into the stone, once more.

With the patience of long practice, Argantel stood before it, as motionless as the Sword. Behind her, footsteps whispered on granite as the others filed in, the black-robed priestesses with their hair unbound, the girls they were training with heads wrapped tightly to protect them from the power. At her back she could feel the cold weight of Ebrdila's glare, as if the older priestess would continue their argument by sheer weight of will.

"You must not do this! Your mother was a greater priestess than you will ever be, and even she did not dare to awaken the Power that sleeps in this Sword! If I were High Priestess, I would never allow you to risk yourself, and the rest of us, this way!"

"But you are not," Argantel had replied. Not for want of trying—but when their Lady died, the priestesses had chosen her daughter to lead them. *"And even if you were, by birth I am the Keeper of this blade."*

"At least leave your cousin out of this. If he knew about this, her father's wrath would strike us all!" It was capitulation, even if Ebrdila did not want to admit it.

"Maderun has the right to be here. The Sword will recognize her and do her no harm. . . ."

Looking across the stone at the younger woman, Argantel hoped that was true. Maderun had been garbed, like herself, in red. Beneath the fall of shining hair her features were pinched with strain, and her eyes flicked uneasily as each new-comer entered the House of the Sword. It was barely large enough for all of them, round, in the ancient fashion, but built of native granite instead of daub and wattle. The walls were low, but the roof timbers met almost thirty feet above her head.

Argantel sent the other girl a pulse of wordless reassurance. Maderun's gray gaze shifted from the Sword to her cousin, and she tried to smile.

The priestess felt a pang of misgiving. She did not doubt her cousin's courage, but she was increasingly aware of the girl's vulnerability. Yet Maderun would have been shamed if Argantel had tried to exclude her now. And it had seemed to her that the God in the Sword might hear the voices of two who came of the blood of its keepers more clearly than one.

As the women entered they moved deosil around the room, and that constant sunwise circling was altering the sense of watchful expectance which Argantel usually felt in this place to an active anticipation. This chamber needed no warding.

Five centuries before, it had been hallowed by priestesses more powerful than any that she would ever know, when Roman legions destroyed the sanctuary on the isle of Mona and the last of the druid priesthood fled northward.

In her grandmother's time it had become something more than a ritual chamber. Her grandmother had brought them the Sword. And what, the priestess wondered, would the Sword bring to them? For fifty years the druids of the Isle of Maidens had preserved it. Each year they had dutifully honored the god who dwelt within. But this ritual was different. This was the first time Argantel had taken it upon herself to ask His aid.

The torches flickered wildly as the great doors were closed. When they had stilled, the priestess nodded to Maderun, who began to sprinkle herbs from her basket across the coals in the brazier before her. In moments their pungent scent filled the room. Smoke spiraled lazily toward the thatching. Argantel took a deep breath, feeling the familiar lift and swing of awareness, as if her ordinary self were being pushed aside to let the persona of the priestess take control.

Maderun's eyes were already unfocused. The priestess smiled a little and reached out with her own awareness until she sensed the younger woman like a blaze of light before her. A little further, and she felt her cousin's spirit awaken within her own. It was not the steady support of a trained priestess, but it was familiar, as though a forgotten piece of herself had just been found.

She let her breath out slowly, releasing her own tension, listening as the other women began to sing. There were no words to it, only tones that built a bridge of ascending harmonies. Slowly she lifted her arms, compelling their attention.

"Behold the Sword of War!" she cried. "God-steel, star-steel, cast flaming down from heaven to bury itself in earth's womb. Spell-steel, forged by Kurdalagon, master of Chalybes's magic. Neither breaking nor bending, neither rusting nor tarnished, this immortal blade we honor!"

"By what right?" called Ebrdila from across the circle, her voice ringing with a sincerity that was more than ritual.

"By right of birth and blood," together, Argantel and Maderun replied. "We are the granddaughters of Rigantona daughter of Gutuator, who came to be high priestess on this holy isle, and of Artorius Hamicus Sarmatius, who was the last priest of the Sword. From the land of the Royal Scyths his fathers brought it, to guard as a holy trust until the time comes when it shall be wielded by a king once more."

"And when shall that king come?" asked one of the other priestesses.

"The God of the Sword shall raise up a king to serve him when his people are in their greatest need," Argantel answered. "And who can doubt our need now? The Eagles have flown, and Britannia's enemies beset her from every side." For a moment she smelled the reek of the burning villa in the smoke from the brazier and her breath caught in her throat.

"It is so—" came the murmured answer. "Call upon the God of the Sword, and we will abide His will."

Maderun, who had been warned, shut her eyes. Argantel swallowed. The next part she did not like, but she had learned to do it. The high gods needed no sacrifice, but the power that lived in the Sword came from an older time. In a wicker cage at the base of the stone a red cock was waiting, victor of many a battle with other champions bred by the men whose fathers had defended Hadrian's Wall. The priestess bent, murmuring, and slid open the door to the cage.

The bird stared about fiercely, but it did not struggle as she drew it forth and held it high. A good sign, for its tattered comb bore witness to the cock's fighting spirit, and the men who handled these birds were accustomed to wear gloves to protect them from sharp beaks and spurs.

"So, my warrior, be still," she murmured, stroking its feathers and feeling the rapid heartbeat gallop beneath her hand. "Here is a more noble death than the cock pit. You shall go undefeated to the god."

The cock's beady eyes fixed on her own, and then, slowly,

closed. Her own eyes stung with mingled exultation and pity, and for a moment she could not move. It would be sacrilege to bungle this, but the cook had made her kill chickens for the pot until she could do it with a merciful efficiency, saying no one should be allowed to eat meat who was not willing to take responsibility for the act that transformed it from living flesh to food. Then she took a quick breath, and twisted, holding tight to the twitching body as the hot blood sprayed across the gray stone.

As the blood flowed she could feel the life leaving, first awareness, and then the energies of the body, and finally an indefinable change that left the cock lighter by more than the weight of its blood. But as the bird became a dead husk in her hands, the stone before her began to pulse with energy.

She laid the body of the cock at the base of the stone, straightened, and lifted her hands; and Maderun, feeling the pulse of power, opened her eyes and raised hers as well.

"Sword-God, War-God, God of Justice, we call you. Cocidius, Red Lord, and Shining Belutacadros we call, as the folk in this land hailed you before the Romans came. Mars of the Soldiers, hear us, and forgive us that we have no knowledge of your other names." She stretched out her hands and set them about the hilt, and Maderun covered them with her own.

Argantel had been taught the secret twist by which the Sword might be withdrawn, but though a woman could guard the blade, it was not for her to wield it. And indeed, as she felt the power focused in the Sword growing, she would not have dared. It was hard enough simply to hold onto it, and she was glad of the strength of Maderun's hands enclosing hers.

"Hear us!" she cried, "as you heard your servants in years of old. Grant us a vision! Show us the Defender who will restore peace to this land!"

She felt Maderun's clasp loosen, freed one hand and gripped her cousin's hard over her own. The younger woman's eyes had closed; she swayed, tremors shaking her body. Argantel suppressed a surge of panic. This wasn't supposed to be happening! Maderun's role was to support, to add her energy, her need, to that of the priestess to whom the God would send His words.

Fool that she was, to think that because her cousin was untrained she had no ability. They shared the same blood and the same potential—and without the disciplines of a priestess, Maderun had no defenses against the force that lived in the Sword.

She moved again, this time trying to detach Maderun's fingers from the hilt. But now it was the other girl who clung with a grip she could not break. Argantel straightened, fighting to control her own breathing as Maderun twitched and moaned.

"Belutacadros!" she cried, choosing the most beneficent of the aspects she knew. "We have called you, and given you honor. Go gently with this woman, daughter of your priests of old. Speak through her, that we may hear, and leave her without harm!"

Very carefully she let go of the Sword and edged backward, lifting her hands in salutation. For a moment longer Maderun jerked, gasping, like a horse that fights the rein. Then she stilled, and the tension went out of her in a long sigh. When the girl drew breath once more, Argantel could *see* how, with the air, something else was flowing into her. Or rather Someone Else, for the figure that held the Sword now stood like a warrior, tall and grim.

"Long . . . it has been long since I wore flesh. . . ." The first words were a whisper, then the voice strengthened. It was deep, with a faintly gutteral accent.

Argantel blinked, for laid like a veil above the form of her cousin she saw a man's shape, clad in a hauberk of overlapping scales, features half-hidden by a helm. For a moment he gazed around the chamber, and the priestesses flinched and bowed their heads, afraid to meet his gaze. Trembling, Argantel held her own head high, praying she would have the courage to face the power she had invoked.

The dark gaze turned to her at last. "Why have you called Me here?"

"My people perish, beset on every side. The Romans forbade us to bear arms, and now they have abandoned us. Send us a Duke of War." He looked at her and suddenly he laughed. It was not a comforting sound.

"You have asked for War and War you shall have. The enemies of whom you now complain are children compared to those who shall come after them."

"What do you mean? Is there nothing we can do?"

"I am a god of Justice. What you ask for you shall receive. If your leaders act in honor, they may yet be saved, but if they are ruled by greed they will lose all. I do not ordain this fate; I only read men's hearts and tell you what I see."

"Then I ask you to give us a King who will rule with honor, a King who will be worthy to wield this Sword!"

For a long moment he looked at her, and the pressure of his gaze forced her to her knees. "He will come," he said softly at last, "not from your womb, but from your blood. You will ally yourself with a husband who is skilled in war and true in heart, and sworn to shed his blood for this land. He will defend the North by force of arms, and you will defend it by the force of the spirit. Tigernissa, High Queen, you shall never be, but *Branuen* I name you, the White Raven of Britannia who rules the hidden realm. You have the will. It remains to be seen whether you have the wisdom. Use your power well."

Argantel felt the color leave her cheeks and then flood back again.

"And what of my cousin, whose body now serves you. What will her fate be?"

"She is an empty vessel, that any power that passes can fill. A wilder power than my own will possess her, nor can you protect her. But from wildness shall come wisdom, and the child she bears must live, for by his magic you shall gain your king."

Once more he glanced around him, and as she heard his voice ringing across the room Argantel realized that his previous words had been for her alone to hear.

"Endure, resist, meet honor with honor, and your Duke of

War shall become a Peace-King whose name will live as long as this land lasts."

He looked back at the Sword, fingering the hilt regretfully. Then, with a little sigh, his eyes closed. For a moment Argantel was not sure who she was seeing. Then it was only Maderun who stood there, dazed and pale, and as Argantel realized that the god had left her, the girl swayed and crumpled to the floor.

"You will ally yourself with a husband who is skilled in war, and true in heart, and sworn to shed his blood for this land."

Beneath her lashes Argantel considered the husband the Sword-God had given her. At least she supposed it must be the work of some god, from the rapidity with which the marriage negotiations had been concluded. Amlodius Licinius, Protector of Brigantia, had the height of his barbarian ancestors, tribesmen from the north coast of Germania who had crossed the Rhenus to enter the service of Rome. His fair skin was reddened by exposure to wind and weather, his pale hair thinning, as if the pressure of a helmet had worn it away. His blunt features bore the marks of a decided character, but she did not yet know if he was kind.

To those who had argued out the marriage contract, that had not been important. What mattered to them was that he represented the last legitimate government established by Rome. As for Amlodius, he recognized that the times were changing, and wished to found a dynasty that would endure in the North by allying himself to the oldest blood in the land. He would respect her birth, and if he did not, she was Lady of the Lake, with her own defenses.

She mopped up some of the meat sauce with a bit of bread and chewed it slowly. She had thoroughly considered all the aspects of this alliance. Amlodius needed her link to the land, and the Old Faith needed a protector. The marriage had the blessing of the gods. The table was strewn with the remains of the wedding feast, and soon it would be time for the bedding. Only now, confronted with the physical reality of her new husband, did she wonder if among all the reasons of state that bound them there might be room for love.

The great hall which had once been the basilica of the Roman magistrates of Luguvalium was garlanded with greenery and crowded with all those who had come to honor the occasion. She supposed she should be flattered, although they had come as much to win favor with Amlodius as to honor her.

Coroticus, newly come to his grandfather's high seat at Dun Breatann in Altacluta, had been given a place at the high table. Flushed with wine, he was debating policy with Vitalinus of Glevum. Vitalinus was as wily, it was said, as the fox from whose pelt he might have taken the color of his hair. Antonius Donatus, Protector of the Novantae country, watched them sourly. He was an old man now, appointed to his post by Theodosius, the last ruler of a united Empire. He had fought the Picts and the Scotii most of his long life, and seen the power of Rome drain away from Britannia like blood from a wound.

At one of the lower tables her cousin Maderun sat with some of the princes' wives. As if she had felt the thought, Maderun looked up and smiled. Smiling back at her, Argantel realized that most of those here were friends to her husband, not to her. Abruptly she found herself wishing she could go down to sit with the other women, and wondering whether anyone at the high table would miss her if she did.

But then she would have had to talk to Ebrdila, who could not quite hide her satisfaction. Argantel remained High Priestess and Lady of the Lake, but at least until Amlodius had got her with child, she must remain in Luguvalium, and the older woman would rule the priestesses in fact, if not in name.

"They say that Ambrosius is dying—"

A sudden tension in the man beside her recalled Argantel's attention. It was Coroticus who had spoken, but everyone was looking at Vitalinus.

"Who will wear the purple after him?" Argantel said then, since no one else seemed willing to ask.

"Does it matter?" asked Coroticus. "The time of the emperors is ended. It was ever the way of our people for each tribe to choose a king, as we do in Alba. Even in Britannia the authority of Ambrosius and the House of Constantine was not everywhere accepted, is that not so?" He looked at Vitalinus again, and Argantel remembered hearing that the Lord of Glevum had opposed Ambrosius to the point of civil war.

"Emperor or overking, the name does not matter," said Vitalinus, pushing away his platter. "But someone must exercise supreme authority. If our people had stood together, Rome would never have conquered us at all." He lifted his goblet, found it empty, and set it down again. Argantel gestured to one of the serving lads to go around the table refilling them.

"I agree," rumbled Amlodius. "Today, Britannia is more than just the British tribes, and the Picts and the Scotii threaten us all. What use is it for me to fight them off here if they then turn their keels northward to attack you, Coroticus, in Dun Breatann? When wolves attack a herd, they separate the weakest animal from the rest and bring it down, but if the others make a ring of defense around it, the attackers can do nothing. We must stand together or they will gobble us up piecemeal."

It was the longest speech she had yet heard from him, thought Argantel. Clearly he was articulate enough in court or camp. She would have to teach him that women were capable of sensible discourse as well.

"My thought exactly!" Vitalinus looked at him gratefully.

"Perhaps such measures are required in the south," objected Coroticus, "where for generations the men of the tribes have been forbidden to bear arms. But the men of the north still know how to use their swords, and we need no emperor who will take more in taxes than the enemy takes in spoils!"

Amlodius shook his head. "There are strong arms in the south—twenty-year men of the Legions who have retired near the old fortresses. They are not British, but this is their home, and they can teach their skills to the sons they have bred up in this land."

"Will you seek to be emperor if Ambrosius dies?" asked old Antonius Donatus.

"I will!" Vitalinus answered, his gaze continuing on to the other men. "Will you support me?"

Amlodius nodded. "I will uphold you, so that you confirm me in my lordship here—" His glance went to Argantel, as if that had reminded him of the other source of his authority.

"I will swear alliance," Coroticus said then, "but my people were never ruled by the South, and will not accept an over-lord."

Antonius Donatus nodded his agreement. "But it is not the men of the North that you must convince to help you defend them, Vitalinus. We love our independence, but the Pictish wolf is always at our door. Your task will be to persuade the great folk of southern Britain, who have lived in peace for so long they cannot believe anyone would dare to do them harm."

"I will persuade them," Vitalinus said soberly. "And I will rule."

Amlodius lifted his goblet in salutation. A silence fell as the others drained their own. Then Antonius Donatus looked at Argantel and laughed.

"Well, this is fine talk for a wedding feast! I wonder that your bride has not fallen asleep waiting for you to pay her some attention."

"I am not sleepy, I assure you," said Argantel tartly. "I saw the ruin the Scotii leave behind them only a few months ago. We women may not take up a sword, but we can die on one. Should we not be as concerned with what plans are being made for our defense as you?"

"Ho, you have married a fire-eater!" Coroticus laughed. "Take care lest you set the bed aflame!"

Argantel was interested to see a flush of embarrassment redden Amlodius's neck and ears.

Some of the other guests, overhearing, were beginning to shout that it was time for the bedding of the bride. Argantel felt her own cheeks grow warm, and wondered if her face were as crimson as her veil. Ebrdila was advancing towards her with Maderun and the other women close behind.

"We will escort the Lady to the bridal chamber," she said grandly, "and inform you when she is ready."

It was like a ritual, thought Argantel as she rose to her feet. All the decisions had been made, and it only remained to go through the ceremonial motions. Wordless, she allowed the other women to lead her out of the hall.

Argantel sat wrapped in a nightrobe in front of the hearth, her waist-length hair spread out across her shoulders like a veil. The other women were busy turning back the bed and arranging the greenery with which they had adorned the room. Maderun drew the brush through the last strand of hair and stepped back, head tipped to admire her handiwork.

"Look how it gleams!" Maderun lifted it so that her cousin could see. Argantel nodded. As Maderun laid the lock back again it shimmered with little fiery glints from the flame on the hearth, reminding her abruptly of the Sword.

"Lord, I consented to this marriage because of your words," she prayed silently, *"grant it your blessing . . ."*

Maderun, misinterpreting her stillness, laid a hand on her shoulder.

"Argantel, are you afraid?"

She shook her head. "I have served the Goddess in the holy rites, and I am not a virgin. It is only that this life will be such a change from all I have known."

Maderun sighed. "That is true for all of us. I used to dream of entering a holy sisterhood, but if what spoke to you in the Sword-rite was a divine being and no demon, we must bear the children Britannia needs. No doubt my father will be arranging a match for me when I get home."

"I suppose so—" Argantel looked up at her cousin, and saw something vulnerable, almost fey, in her expression. The other women were already moving toward the door. Filled with sudden tenderness, she took the other girl's hand and kissed it. "Thank you, Maderun, for staying to support me on this day. May your god bless and protect you on your journey home."

Maderun caught Argantel's hand to her cheek and smiled.

"And may your goddess fill your new husband with love for you." She smiled tremulously and, turning, followed the others from the room.

Argantel was not left long alone.

Barely a moment had passed, it seemed, when the door was flung open again and the men, laughing, thrust Amlodius into the room.

"Be off with you, now! You have seen us put together in the bridal chamber. Go get drunk or something, and leave us alone!"

Propelled by a volley of bawdy commentary, the door slammed shut. Amlodius drew a deep breath, some of the high color leaving his face. Clutching her robe closed, Argantel rose. She was a tall woman, but he towered over her.

He cleared his throat. "We have not had much time to become acquainted, but I will try to be a good husband to you. You must tell me if there is something you need."

She nodded. "Most of all I will need you to talk to me. I have been used to ruling the priestesses on the Isle of Maidens, as you rule your warriors here. Do not treat me like a woman who knows no more than her distaff and her cookfire, Amlodius. Like you, I serve this land. Do we have an agreement?" She paused. "You are looking at me as if you were surveying a battlefield."

Amusement sparked in his blue eyes, and as he shrugged off his robe, she saw that if this was a combat, his forces were ready. Argantel felt a slow fire kindling beneath her skin.

"That bed is our field, lady, and you shall be my fellow-warrior. . . ."

With a swift step he bore down upon her, and letting her own garment fall, she readied herself for the fray.

†HE WÎLÐ MAП

A·D· 425—29

†HE ROAD FROM LUGUVALIUM TO DEVA RAN SOUTH THROUGH THE hills and then straight across the levels beside the sea. In these times no route could be said to be completely secure, but after what she had seen the preceding autumn, Maderun feared to return to Maridunum by sea.

The weather grew warmer as Beltain neared. Creamy primroses clustered beneath the hedges and the first starry blooms of the hawthorne appeared. As each day came to a peaceful close, the fear that had made Maderun tense against each jolt of the horse-litter faded and she began to enjoy the journey. She had never, she thought, known the land to be so beautiful. She laughed at the antics of the new lambs on the hillsides, and plaited the flowers that the men of her escort picked for her into wreaths for their hair. Maderun listened to their singing and laughed, for it was the tune that the lads and lasses sang when they went out to gather greenery for Beltain.

Two weeks of journeying brought them in sight of the northern coast of the old Deceangli lands that curved west into the sea. Here the road ran between the water and the forest. Another long day's journey would bring them to Deva, and a bath, thought Maderun longingly, and a soft bed.

Looking around their campsite, no one would guess that a

major center of Roman civilization lay so near. Tonight she would lack even the poor comforts of a shepherd's shelter. Since noon they had passed only one ruined farmstead. The men were already busy cutting branches to build her a leafy bower. However, they had water and firewood, and the evening was calm and beautiful. She watched the sun go down across the Hibernian Sea and knew herself at peace with the world.

Peace there might be in field and forest, but it was otherwise in the world of men. Just before dawn, Maderun found herself sitting up in her blankets, wondering what had awakened her. She looked around for the warrior on watch and could not see him. Alarm burned the last of the sleep from her brain and she drew breath to call out a warning, and in that instant the darkness exploded.

Sword blades flared red as someone kicked the coals and the banked fire burst into new flame. Maderun heard a grunt and one of the struggling bodies fell; warm blood splattered her hand. She gasped and struggled to her feet. *Scottii raiders . . .* the thought came through the gibbering in her brain. *But the sea had been empty. Where had they come from?*

Clutching the blanket around her, she tried to distinguish friend from foe. In the growing light she saw that several of her escort were down. The others were too few to hold all of the raiders, some of whom were already beginning to paw through the piles of gear.

One of them caught sight of her and grinned, and Maderun remembered with appalling clarity the burned villa and the body of the little girl. As the Scot started towards her the horror that had frozen her limbs became a hot tide of terror and she ran.

She fled like a frightened doe, blundering into branches and stumbling over roots and stones. When she came to a halt at last, breathless and bleeding from a dozen scratches, she heard crashing in the undergrowth behind her, and compelled her trembling legs to carry her onward.

When fear-begotten strength finally failed, Maderun forced

her slim body through a hole some creature had made in the tangled lower branches of a hazel copse and lay still. Whether she fainted then or only slept she did not know. But when she became aware once more it was full daylight, and in the forest there were no sounds but the musical gurgle of a nearby stream and the cheerful morning song of the birds.

She had lost the blanket, and the undergown in which she had slept was dirty and torn. But at least no one was pursuing her. Slowly, for overstressed muscles had stiffened and she ached in every limb, she crawled out of the hazels and down to the stream. The cool water eased her thirst, and bathed some of the hurt from her face and arms. She sat up then, looking around her, and realized that she had no idea where she might be.

Argantel would know how to find her way out of the forest, she told herself, looking around her. *What would she do now?* Water ran toward the ocean, she thought, and the road ran beside it. She had only to follow the stream.

But perhaps in her panic she had run south instead of east, or perhaps it was only that the forest brook meandered where it chose, in no hurry to reach the sea. Maderun was still lost when darkness fell on the forest—and hungry, for aside from a few greens whose leaves she recognized, she had found nothing to eat all day. Weeping a little from fatigue and hunger, she curled up between the gnarled roots of a great oak tree.

Maderun woke once in the night, whimpering from a dream of terror; finding herself safe and warm, she dropped swiftly into sleep once more. When she woke again she sensed light through her closed eyelids. She started to move and winced. What had she been doing yesterday to get so sore? She remembered men fighting, and a terrified flight through the forest, but surely that had been in her nightmare, because now she lay in a warm bed. . . .

Her eyes opened. Above her light filtered through green leaves. But the air was quite still. She listened, and realized that what she had taken for the wind was the sound of someone breathing. Her groping fingers closed on fur. She jerked upright, turning, and found herself staring down into a flat, wide-nostriled face. Brown hair thick as a bear's pelt grew low above a pair of dark eyes.

Maderun gasped and started to scramble away. A long-fingered hand, attached to a sinewy arm which was also covered with hair, reached out and grasped her ankle. The grip was not tight enough to hurt, but quite secure. She could not get away.

Swallowing her fear, Maderun looked at her captor. If the beast had meant to eat her she would be dead already. She saw long legs, and feet very like those of a man, a thick barrel, and—she looked quickly away. He—not it—was unmistakably male, but not quite a beast. Seeing him whole, she recognized the original of the distorted masks and tunics of tufted wool in which men cavorted at festivals. It was a Wild Man.

She had been told they were all dead, or at least withdrawn to the far northern lands. What was one doing here? Around his face white hairs sprinkled the dark fur. Was he the last in Britannia?

She searched her memory for the old tales. The Wildfolk were shy creatures, but could fight fiercely if captured. At times they had rescued lost children and cared for them until they were found. That gave her hope. She licked dry lips and pointed to the stream.

The Wild Man chuffed deep in his throat and released her ankle. Carefully she made her way to the brookside and cupped water in her hands to drink. Then she made her way behind a clump of sallow to relieve herself, still uncomfortably aware of his watchful gaze. But when she tried to go further he half rose, growling deep in his throat until she turned back.

Later that morning the Wild Man left her and she tried to escape once more, but he found her when she was scarcely out of sight of the oak tree and carried her back under his arm. Some tender roots and new greens lay on the ground beside the tree root, and a piece of honeycomb. Still weeping, Maderun ate greedily.

* * *

The infant moon began to wax with little change in Made-run's captivity. By day she followed the Wild Man, learning which plants could be eaten. By night she slept warm in his arms. She grew thin on a diet of tubers and raw greens, and wept again when the grubs and raw birds' eggs the Wild Man brought began to look good to her. She tried to pray for deliverance, but prayers to the Christian god seemed irrelevant here in the wildwood, and she had never learned how to address the old gods of her tribe. Argantel would have known. "Cousin, help me!" she cried, but her only answer was the wind in the trees.

To think about her situation brought pain, and so as the days passed she avoided thought and banished memory, taking refuge in the forest's eternal *now*. To live was to feel the warmth of the sun or the cool wind, the satisfaction of food in the belly and the sweetness of water on the tongue. Wordless, she seemed to sense the life that flowed through all the green world around her in a way she had only glimpsed when she was part of the world of men.

Bright eyes gleamed through the sparkle of a waterfall; willowy maidens emerged from the trunks of their trees to dance in the moonlight, and once, just at sunset, she glimpsed the turf of a forgotten mound opening like a door, and saw a radiant figure that beckoned to her to come in. She might have gone, but her captor, growling deep in his throat, had grasped her arm and dragged her away.

The Wild Man had a territory through which he ranged, gathering the sweet onion in one place, mustard in another, fish from a forest pool, grubs from beneath a fallen log. It took most of his time and energy just to find enough food to support his giant frame. Maderun tore off the ragged hem of her skirt, and clad now in what was no more than a short tunic, followed him. They slept sometimes in a hollow tree and at others in a kind of nest lined with soft grasses, but always they returned to the oak tree by the stream.

The moon grew full and round, blessing the woodlands with

her silver light. In the world of men, if Maderun had had any way to calculate the calendar, it was the moon when men and women danced together around the Beltain fires. In the forest, Maderun lay curled beneath her captor's hand as once she had curled around her pet kitten. The Wild Man stroked her as she had touched her cat, drawing his long, lightly furred fingers through her hair and humming tunelessly as he often did at such times. She held still when he sniffed along her body, nostrils flaring. Sometimes he licked her skin and she shivered, simultaneously repulsed and pleasured. In this state of mindless endurance, it seemed inevitable that one day his touch should grow more intimate, and when he thrust her down and dog-fashion, entered her, she did not try to pull away.

While the moon remained full this usage continued. In that corner of her mind that still could think Maderun knew that reason was her enemy. If she allowed herself to understand what was happening, she would be reduced to gibbering hysteria. And if she recognized that she had come to welcome it her mind would snap entirely.

When the silver round began to thin, the Wild Man seemed to lose interest, though he fed and protected her as before. One night, when the moon was only a thin sickle in the sky, Maderun dreamed. She was looking in a mirror, and then she realized it was not a mirror but Argantel who was facing her, calling her name. And when she replied, the other woman cried, *"Remember the hope of Britannia! Remember the Sword!"*

When she woke, Maderun knew herself as human for the first time in many days. But she scarcely recognized the gaunt features that stared back at her from the forest pool. *If I stay here, I will die*, she thought, and then, *Better to die than to live as an animal. . . .*

The Wild Man was watching her, his dark eyes sorrowful as if he sensed her unhappiness, but Maderun refused to pity him. She no longer feared him, nor did their strange life together disgust her, but from that time she began to actively try to recover her humanity.

It was three days later that she heard in the distance the

melancholy belling of a hunter's horn. The Wild Man was off somewhere, seeking food. Heart pounding, Maderun set off toward the sound of the horn. For a time she waded in the stream, hoping to throw him off the scent if he should follow her. Then she took to the bank once more, moving as swiftly as she dared.

The horns grew louder, and she heard the yapping of hounds. But closer still she heard a familiar deep chuffing and knew that the Wild Man was coming after her. Her first cry was a squawk, and for one panicked moment she wondered if she had forgotten how to form human words. Then she filled her lungs and tried again.

"Help—help me!"

For a moment there was silence, then she heard a change in the calling of the hounds. Rapidly they drew closer, but the Wild Man was gaining too. Panting, Maderun leaped for the lower branches of a gnarled apple tree, survivor of some forgotten orchard, and began to climb, seeking the topmost branches that would bear her slender weight but not that of her pursuer. Clinging to the bough she cried out again and again.

The Wild Man splashed through the stream and paused at the foot of Maderun's tree. For a long, wordless moment she stared into his eyes. Then the yammering of the dogs grew deafening and he crouched to meet them, the rough hair over neck and shoulders rising to a crest as he bared his teeth.

"Run!" cried Maderun, gesturing towards the undergrowth. "Run, or they will kill you!"

Once more the Wild Man looked up, jaws opening in a very human moan. Then, as the first of the dogs leaped through the undergrowth, he whirled away into the forest and was gone.

Let the hunters think that the dogs had treed her, thought Maderun as they milled around the base of the beech, whining. Let them think that her tears were from fear of them, and not because now, when she was sure of rescue, she could at last afford to pity the creature that was more than a beast, if less than a man, and who in his way had loved her.

* * *

To her rescuers, Maderun would say only that she had wandered in the wildwood, living on roots and greens, meeting no man. Her father received her with astonished joy, for her marriage had figured in his plans. But she continued to weep, and so he sent her for healing to the quiet confines of the convent next to the church of Saint Peter in the town.

The nuns were kind to her, and if their garden was not quite so peaceful as the forest, it was far better than the smoky clamor of her father's hall. Maderun sank gratefully into the routine of song and prayer, and her memories of the wildwood became as faint and disjointed as images in a dream.

When her bleeding did not come at the change of the moon, the Infirmary sister patted her hand kindly and assured her that when a woman had suffered a shock or was as thin as Maderun had become, it was often so. With good food and rest, surely she would grow healthy once more. And indeed, as the summer passed, she began to fill out a little, though her face was still gaunt and pale. But her moon blood did not return.

She dreamed, sometimes, that she was back in the forest. Sometimes she relived the terror of that first flight from the raiders, and would wake in a cold sweat, babbling of blood and monsters among the trees. But sometimes her dreams returned her to the oak tree, and she smiled, thinking she still slept cradled in the Wild Man's arms. Those were the times when she reached out to him, and writhing on her narrow bed, touched herself as *he* had touched her, until she passed into peaceful sleep once more. The other girls in the novices' dormitory would ask her what she had been dreaming, but Maderun could not answer them.

On a warm autumn day just after the Feast of St. Michael, Maderun went out with a few of the older nuns and the three novices to gather apples.

"Have you heard?" said little Felicia as they searched for windfalls among the tall grass, "Ambrosius the Emperor is dead and Vitalinus of Glevum has proclaimed himself Vor-Tigernus—High King!"

"And how would you know that?" asked Thea, the brown-skinned daughter of a legionary from Numidia who had married a British woman and settled in Demetia when his term of service was done. "Did an angel announce it to you in a dream?" The folklore of the convent was rich in tales of supernatural visitors.

"I heard it in Maridunum, of course," retorted Felicia, "when I accompanied Sister Ildeg to market last Saturday."

"God prosper him," put in the third girl. "For well He knows how much we need a strong lord. But I do not think that the chieftains of the West Country will accept Vitalinus's rule."

The others nodded. They were all, if not the daughters of princes, girls of good family. And in the West, even the poorest hill farmer felt free to criticize the doings of those who claimed authority over him.

Thea laughed. "Of course not—it is Ambrosius Aurelianus who has the right to claim his father's honors."

"But he is still in Armorica with his brother. My father says we need a king who will care for Britannia first and foremost," Felicia replied. "Vitalinus doesn't want to be emperor. He titles himself in our own language, *'over king.'* "

Maderun nodded. "I met him at the wedding of my cousin in Luguvalium. He seemed a very determined man."

The others looked at her in surprise, unaccustomed to hearing her speak and remembering now that she outranked them all.

"He will need to be," Felicia said finally. "He is trying to raise an army, and our men will not want to fight for people at the other end of the country when the Dalriadan warriors are at our door."

Maderun shuddered, remembering the raiders, and the others fell abruptly silent.

"They say that is why Vitalinus claimed the power—" Felicia added softly. "Because of what happened to you. He has said it is a disgrace that a princess of a royal house cannot travel safely through the land, and Britannia needs a defender."

"A Defender . . ." Maderun spoke softly in the cadence of prophecy, recalling fragments of the knowledge that had passed through her awareness, it seemed a lifetime ago, "but it will not be the Vor-Tigernus, but another, who shall come after him."

"What?" asked Thea, but Maderun shook her head, losing the memory. This had happened to her often since her ordeal. She lived in the present; all her memories were like fragments of dream, and as easily whirled away.

"We have gathered all the windfalls," Felicia said brightly into the silence. "And for all our shaking, no more apples will fall out of this tree. But there are still some clinging to the upper branches. They are almost ripe, and it seems a shame to leave them there."

Maderun looked up, dimly remembering that trees meant safety. "I will go after them. I am the lightest of you all." Kirtling up her skirts, she began to clamber upward.

From the top of the tree she could see over the convent walls. She could see the roofs of Maridunum, and beyond them a patchwork of field and forest. But inevitably her gaze turned northward, where the land disappeared into a blue haze, and the wind dried the tears that sprang beneath her eyelids before she could wipe them away.

"Can you reach the apples?" the call came from below.

Recalled to the present, Maderun stretched to grasp the fruit, and the wind flattened her gown against her body and blew back her hair.

There was a stifled exclamation from below. Maderun plucked an apple and settled back, turning to look down. Felicia was staring up at her wide-eyed.

"What is wrong?"

"Daughter of Carmelidus, I think you go with child!"

The apple slipped from Maderun's grasp, missed the basket, and rolled across the grass. Only a convulsive tightening of her arms saved her from falling as well. She shook her head and reached for another apple, then picked a third and two more.

By the time she climbed back down the tree, Maderun could almost believe she had not heard it. But the flushed faces and avid eyes of the other girls forced her to remember Felicia's words.

"It is not so—" she said quietly. "I have never lain with a man."

"But your breasts are so round, and your belly—"

"Hush!" said Thea, taking pity on her. "If she is a maiden, then time will proclaim her innocence, and time will accuse her more harshly than any man if it is not so. It is not for us to judge."

It is not true. . . . Maderun repeated to herself as they carried their baskets back to the convent. *I have never loved a man.*

But as Thea had said, time did indeed accuse her—time, and the wagging tongues of two dozen cloistered women, who began to watch Maderun's belly as a farmer scans his newly sown field. And by Samhain it was apparent to everyone that the princess was expecting a child.

Then the questioning began.

"It is a great sorrow, but no shame to you, child, if one of the Scottii raiders who attacked your camp caught and raped you before you fled," said Mother Paterna.

"They were still busy fighting. I got away."

And indeed, the evidence of Maderun's maidservant, who had rolled under a pile of luggage and watched till the fight was over, did seem to confirm that when Maderun ran, the men who followed returned quickly, complaining that she had gotten away.

"Escaped slaves and outlawed men take refuge in the wilderness. If it was one of these who abused you, tell me, and we will hunt him down!" said her father.

"I ate at no hearth and met no human soul from the time I fled to the day that I was found," answered Maderun, and it was true, said some, that even outlaws would not have allowed the girl to live in such a condition as she had been found.

"Why will you not believe me?" she cried. "Put me to the ordeal, let me swear on holy relics that I have not lied to you!"

And she swore, and was not blasted, and so her accusers were no closer to the truth than before. In the convent they whispered that if she had lain with no man in the wilderness perhaps something worse had come to her then, or even—and here the voices of the novices grew faint with excitement—within the convent walls.

"We will wait until the child is born," they said then. "Whether its father be man or devil, the babe itself will proclaim its paternity."

And so Maderun's pregnancy continued through the winter. Her belly grew ever larger, and the older women counted the months, nodding wisely. But the ninth month since Maderun's rescue passed, and there was no child. The whispers changed then, to talk of the incubus who lies with women in their sleep, or the Devil himself, seeking to beget an Anti-Christ into the world.

"Perhaps it is so," said Maderun wearily above the great round of her belly, "for indeed I sometimes have strange dreams. . . ." But the next day she was talking of a prince of the faerie folk whom she had met in the forest, who had fed her on cakes made from sunbeams and moonlight wine. And that might be so as well, the gossip ran, for the girl had been starving when they found her and surely faerie food, like faerie gold, would vanish in the ordinary light of day.

The bishop heard of the case and sent one of his priests, a Father Blaise, to question her, but if Maderun told the truth to him, the seal of the confessional protected it.

Maderun's child was born at Beltain, when the folk of faerie come forth from their mounds and move from winter quarters to their summer homes. But it was no faerie child she gave birth to, for when he arrived, after a nightlong labor in which the midwives almost despaired of saving either mother or child, he was large, lusty, and covered with a fine pelt of dark down.

"The Devil's child," said one of the midwives, listening to him squall.

"*My* child—" whispered Maderun. "Give him to me!"

They exchanged worried glances, for they had meant to carry the babe away to the forest and leave it there. Exposure of unwanted children was forbidden to Christians, but this, surely, was no Christian babe.

But Maderun was a king's daughter, and though she had babbled strangely during the labor, she spoke with authority now, and so they shrugged and gave her the child. But the rumors did not cease from flying, and when storms ruined the harvest that summer, and gave way to a freezing winter, and the next two years were seasons of little rain, folk began to murmur that it was because the King of Demetia was harboring a witch-daughter and her demon child.

Maderun sat in the convent garden watching her boy playing in the sun. From the little church came the sound of chanting; Maderun leaned back against the cool stone and let the sound carry her spirit upward. After Ambros's birth she had asked to be admitted as a novice, but although she was still welcome to dwell among the nuns, the bishop had forbidden formal vows to the mother of such a dubious child. Perhaps it was for the best, she thought dreamily. She had recovered her health, but she found it hard to concentrate, and could never seem to remember the prayers.

Ambros was squatting on the path, making patterns with the pebbles he found there, his dark hair, coarse as a horse's mane, hanging over his eyes. After his birth most of the fuzz that covered his body had fallen out, except for a line of black down that followed his spine. Carefully he made a circle, and then a square, and other figures, over and over again.

Sometimes he raged, and raced in circles until he was exhausted, but on other days he could play such games for hours. Though he was nearly three, he had never yet spoken a word, but as he worked he hummed softly. The sound made her feel soft and sleepy, and she found it familiar, but could never think where she had heard such humming before.

A winged shadow flickered across the path. The child looked up at the wren that had made it and laughed. Maderun watched in astonishment as the bird fluttered down to alight on his outstretched hand. The wren chirped, and Ambros chirped back at it. Then it took fright suddenly and flew away.

Ambros sat up, dark eyes fixed on the path. Only then did Maderun hear the footsteps and see Father Blaise approaching them. His hair, as always, stood half on end, so that he reminded one of a startled bird, and his step hesitated as he peered nearsightedly around him. But his face was uncharacteristically grim.

"What has happened?" She rose to meet him.

"Three landowners whose hayfields were washed out last summer have brought suit to try you for a witch and sorceress because of the child!"

Maderun made a hushing motion. Because Ambros did not speak, people often did not realize how much he could understand. Then the sense of what the priest had said sank in and she sat down.

"Why?" she whispered. "What harm have I done to them? Surely I am as good a Christian as any woman in this land."

"You will not name the father of your child."

"I cannot—" Sometimes Maderun remembered him as a shining youth and sometimes as a comforting presence in the dark, but she knew that he had no human name.

"God send they will believe it. They have brought the case before their kindred court and the *caput gentis* has chosen Uethen son of Maclovius to judge it, so your father has no power to gainsay them. You must think of something to tell them, Maderun. They have the power to drown you, do you understand?"

She looked at Ambros, and for a moment saw in her mind's eye moonlight sparkling on a forest stream. Then the picture darkened. "I don't remember. . . ."

* * *

Ambros, who was having one of his quiet days, sat on his mother's lap, surveying the scene with eyes as bright and dark as a young bird's. Even though the sky was cloudy, the court had been convened in the meadow beyond the king's hall, the only place large enough to hold so many. The people made a circle, chattering. On the isle of Mona, they whispered, a cow had dropped a two-headed calf. In Londinium, Vitalinus, despairing of building a fighting force from the men of the South and East of Britannia, had followed the ancient tradition of Rome and hired Saxon mercenaries from across the sea.

A damp wind fluttered veils and mantles. Maderun shivered. Once, she thought, there had been someone who would have protected her—a mighty presence who had kept her safe and warm.

Uethen son of Maclovius settled himself on a bench on the hill. His robes were white, but his cloak was woven in many colors, his right as a man who knew the law. He draped the folds more majestically and cleared his throat.

"I call Maderun daughter of Carmelidus into this court—" His voice, trained and resonant, carried clearly, and Maderun felt a changing tension in Ambros's body as he stilled, listening.

She tried to speak, and could not. She knew this feeling of being helpless—the other time, it had been no use to struggle. She shook her head, feeling awareness begin to slip away like an unmoored boat that the current will carry downstream.

Father Blaise, beside her, responded, "She is here."

Uethen nodded. "Who brings suit against her?"

One of the farmers stepped forward. "I bring suit against the daughter of Carmelidus on the charge of *maleficium*, in that she willingly gave herself to the Devil in order to bring his child into the world, who has tampered with the order of nature and brought us nothing but disaster since that day!"

A murmur of interest swept the crowd and all eyes turned toward Maderun.

"That is two accusations!" exclaimed Father Blaise. "I can

bring witnesses to testify that the child was born in a normal manner, and duly baptised when he was three days old. The good nuns of Saint Peter's have watched him grow, and seen him do no magic. If the weather has been bad, it is not his doing. Have you known no other seasons of disaster, when there was no babe to blame? It is for your sins that God has brought this upon you, not his!"

The babble this time was louder, and once or twice she heard laughter.

"It may be so," said the second farmer. "But it does not absolve Maderun of *her* crime. Whether the father be demon or mortal, she has brought dishonor on her kindred by having a nameless child."

"He has the name with which he was baptised," said Father Blaise, "which is Ambrosius, after the emperor."

"And where is the rest of it? Of whom is he the son?"

"He is the child of the nun. And that would be enough among the northern folk from whom this girl's mother came."

"But this is Demetia, and we hold by our own law," said the judge. "If the whoredom of a girl of the kindred dishonors her people, then that of the daughter of a king brings shame upon the whole kingdom, and she must pay the penalty."

"Will you kill *your* mother?"

The question was voiced in a clear and piping tone that carried to the edge of the crowd. Only slowly did men realize that its source was the child who sat in his mother's arms.

"What did you say?" Uethen was staring as if he thought Maderun had played some trick, but in truth she was as surprised as anyone. Could Ambros know what he was saying? Certainly the case had been discussed in his hearing, but how could he understand?

"Your mother doesn't say who *your* father was," Ambros repeated with patient clarity. "Do you drown her too?"

"My father was my mother's husband!" the judge exclaimed.

"How do you know? Do you ask her?"

The first shocked astonishment was giving way to laughter.

Somehow, Ambros's question had turned the temper of the crowd toward sympathy.

"That's so, Uethen—it's not fair to condemn the boy's mother until you know about your own! Send for her, man, and let us all hear."

Uethen was flushing angrily, but he could interpret the murmurs around him. People respected his learning, but he was not a popular man. Someone had already gone to fetch his mother. Glowering, he agreed to wait until she should come.

When the woman arrived, escorted by a grinning warrior, Ambros straightened.

"I do not know my father. I know my mother, and they want to kill her. Does your son know his father?" The tone was clear, wistful. The old woman looked at the child and all saw her eyes fill with tears.

"Ah, little one, there's no man born that can be certain of more." She sighed, and looked up at her son. "It is glad I am that my husband is not here this day, for I came to love him. But he was not the father of my child."

The face of the judge set like stone, and the people whispered, divided between shock and glee. His mother looked at him once, and then away.

"It is our law that a stranger who lies with a girl of the kindred must stay and marry her. But my lover was thirsty for learning, and when he had learned all there was to know of Maridunum, he went away. When I knew that he had left me with child I gave myself to Maclovius, who had long courted me, and so I got a husband." She sighed. "If I may speak in your Assembly I counsel mercy, for Maderun at least has practiced no deception."

There was a long silence, while all eyes turned back to the judge, who had drawn his mantle over his head in mourning.

"I cannot judge this case," he said harshly. "The king is your father, woman. Let him deal with your shame!"

King Carmelidus pushed through the crowd, followed by his house-guard, the high color returning to his face as the tension left it.

"My daughter shall have a husband, and her child a father, as good as yours! Matauc Morobrin has consented to wed her." One of the warriors came forward to stand beside him.

Maderun looked at him, ordinary as bread and solid as stone, and felt the last of her bright dreams mist away. But her child had been saved, for whatever future God, or the old gods, had in mind. Ambros tugged at her gown. With a sigh, she put him to the breast. Upon her head, like a blessing, she felt the first drops of rain.

III

THE RED DRAGON
AND THE WHITE

A.D. 433

THE BALL, MADE FROM A CALF STOMACH STUFFED WITH HAY, HUR-
tled through the air. Ambros, who was faster than the others
though he was only seven, darted beneath Dinabu's arm and
whacked it with his hurley stick as it fell. He straightened to
watch as it arced over the other boy's head toward the goal.

"Curse you, that was *my* ball!" cried Dinabu.

"But it is a point for *our* team—" answered Ambros, watching the other boy warily. He had attempted to play with the
boys before. It usually ended in a quarrel, but he knew how
much it mattered to his mother that he be accepted, and so he
continued to try.

The others began to yell as the ball smacked into the bush
that was serving as goal, and the horsemen who had paused
to watch them play set up a cheer.

Ambros hung back as the ball was put in play once more,
aware with all his senses of the pattern that was emerging, the
energy of the other players, even the life in the grass. He had
learned, painfully, that other people did not sense these things,
and so he tried to hide his knowledge. Sometimes he thought
his mother felt things also, but she did not seem to be aware
of what she knew.

The ball spun toward him. He could see Dinabu running, and knew in the same moment that the older boy would not get there in time. The others were shrieking encouragement. Dinabu would be angry if Ambros hit the ball, but *they* would be pleased. Before he had completed the thought he was moving, placing himself in the correct relationship to ball and goal. Muscles flexed as the stick swung; he felt the vibration all the way up his arm as it struck the ball, the sweet "rightness" as he continued to turn, and the ball soared straight for the goal.

Dinabu turned on him, features contorting. Ambros saw the hurley stick whip toward his head and ducked. Fury reddened his own vision; like a thing foreordained, he could sense how his own blow would strike the other boy's head. With a final effort at control he let go of the stick and saw it whirl away. Dinabu struck again; Ambros plucked the wooden shaft from his grasp and sent it after his own. Dinabu grabbed for his arm, and Ambros danced away, knowing that if they came to grips his own anger would overwhelm him.

"Bastard . . ." panted the older boy, stumbling after him. "No-fathered, demon begotten—"

Ambros avoided his attacks and shut out his words. He had heard it all before. But the other boys, with the pack-mentality of their kind, were taking up the chant, even those on his own team.

"Go away," they cried. "We'll have no devil-child on our side!" Someone picked up a clod of earth and threw.

Ambros knew it would hit him, but held his ground. The tears that smarted in his eyes were of rage.

"You'll ask me—you'll beg me for my help one day!" he growled.

Then, ignoring the insults and the clods that followed him, Ambros stalked away. At the edge of the field a stand of hazels marked the beginning of the woodlands. There was no one in Maridunum who could follow him once he was among the trees.

His rage carried him farther than he had intended. He came to rest at last where water from an unfailing spring trickled down over rock to form a small pool. He bent over it to drink and remained, watching his image take shape as the ripples stilled. Eyes as dark and watchful as a beast's gazed back at him beneath the fall of coarse hair. His brows were heavy, his forehead low. He tried to smile, and large teeth snarled back at him from a heavy jaw. Only in his high arched nose did he resemble his mother's kin.

But I am no child of the Devil, for the priests say that when he comes to tempt humankind his face is fair, and I am as ugly as a hobgoblin. But the hobgoblin was a little fellow, and it was clear already that Ambros was going to be a very big man. *Whatever I am, it is nothing human,* he thought unhappily. *Perhaps I should run away and live in the forest. I am happy here.*

He had considered this before, many times, and always it was the thought of his mother's pain that prevented him from running away. Morobrin was not unkind, but there was no love between them. Maderun and little Ganeda, the girl-child she had borne her new husband, were the only human creatures Ambros loved.

He gazed around him, looking for the other being that cared for him. He used to think she was the spirit of the waterfall, for he had first seen her here. But he had found that if he unfocused his eyes in a certain way he could see her elsewhere, just as he saw the beings that lived in rock and bush and tree. And sometimes, just lately, he would hear her talking to him even when he could not see.

"Girl . . ." he whispered, "will I ever find friends?"

And in the silence of his spirit he heard, faint but clear, *"I am your friend, and I am always here. . . ."*

He lay back upon the bracken and then for a little while he must have slept, lulled by the sweet singing of the waterfall, for when he sat up again, the sky was growing gold.

When he set out for home it was already dark beneath the trees. But Ambros seemed to have eyes in his feet, so swiftly did he go. He was never clumsy in the forest, only in the hall.

*   *   *

Ambros came over the hill to Lys Morobrin as the first stars were kindling in a purple sky. His nostrils flared at the scents of woodsmoke and roasting meat. He began to run, slowing only when he noticed the three strange horses in the pen. They were fine beasts; he frowned, memory supplying an image of them saddled and mounted. They belonged to the men who had been watching the hurley game. What were they doing here?

He doused his head in the horse-trough, combing back his hair with his fingers in an attempt to bring it to some kind of order, but as he thrust aside the spotted cowhide that curtained the doorway he had an unhappy feeling that he had only suc-ceeded in making it stand up in spikes like a bogle's. And his tunic was torn; he had not noticed that before.

Something stirred in the shadows of the entry. Ambros whirled, then relaxed, sensing, even as his eyes adjusted, that it was little Ganeda who was hiding there. He bent and took her into his arms.

"Guests, with pretty clothes!" She pointed into the hall.

"Who are they, sweetling?" Her soft hair, pale as duckling's down, tickled his nose and he set her down again.

"They asked for you," she said, "to bring you honor! Come and see!" She took his hand and pulled him into the center of the hall.

His stepfather and the strangers lay at their ease on dining-couches on the other side of the fire. His mother looked up from her embroidery as he entered, as if that breath of air had alerted her. Maderun was vague about many things, but sur-prisingly alert where her son was concerned. With one glance she took in his appearance and shook her head with a sigh. In another moment she would try to hustle him out to put on his good tunic, but before she could rise, Morobrin spied him and pointed.

Ambros, still standing in the doorway, found himself the target of all eyes. Flushing, he stood his ground.

"That is the boy?" asked one of the strangers, a tall man with a grizzled beard.

"Ambros," said Morobrin, "child of the nun."

"She will have to come with him," said the other man, "to tell her story."

"Where?" Ambros found his voice at last. "Where are we going?"

"To Vitalinus, to the Over-King."

"The king has promised gold and a bull from his own herds if you can help him," said Maderun as they rode northward. "Your father is very pleased. . . ."

He is not my father, thought Ambros, *and he is pleased to be rid of me. You are chattering, mother—what is the knowledge you are trying to hide?*

He knew already that the Over-King's messengers had not told the whole truth to him. They said that a fatherless child was required to bless the king's new fortress, but what if he failed? Ambros did not believe that his mother would knowingly lead him into danger, but she was very good at seeing only those parts of a picture that fitted her vision of reality.

She even thought *he* was handsome, and Ambros knew full well he was as ugly as Imacdub who was the ugliest boy ever born. The goddess Cerituend had brewed up a cauldron of magic to make her son wise if he could not be beautiful, but the serving-lad Viaun had drunk it all instead.

Perhaps my mother's cousin Argantel could teach me wisdom—I have heard she is a mistress of magic, but I think I will have to be Imacdub and Viaun both if I am to survive.

But whatever happened to him in the Over-King's hall, it would be a change from listening to the taunts of the lads at Maridunum, and the little girl who talked to him in his head had told him he should go. He turned to look at the road behind him. The town was already hidden behind a wooded ridge, and they were passing through the last of the farmsteads.

"I met Vitalinus once, you know," his mother chattered on.

"Who?" Lost in his own thoughts Ambros tried to pick up the thread again.

"That is his name. Vor-Tigernus is only the title he has taken, though I suppose it might be courteous to use it when you address him." She frowned. "He did not seem over-weeningly proud, as I remember, but he did have a great many opinions. . . . Great lords do not like to be contradicted—" She turned to Ambros again. "Be careful how you speak to him, but remember that your blood is as good as his."

On one side, thought Ambros unhappily, but he nodded.

"And perhaps," she went on, "it would be better not to tell him about the Sword."

He turned to her. "That will be easy. You have never more than mentioned it to me!"

His mother's face brightened. She liked to tell stories about the past—it was safely over and done. Sometimes, though, the past was like an adder that seems dead until it rolls over and bites you.

"Two hundred years ago there was an emperor in the lands of the Romans who was called Marcus Aurelius." Maderun glanced up and down the road and decided that the riders in their escort were out of earshot. "In his time there was war between the Sarmatian peoples beyond the borders of Dacia, and one of the losing tribes, the Iazyges, came to the Danuvius and asked for asylum in the Empire. The emperor replied that he could not take all of them together, but if they were willing to be divided, he would let them in.

"Five hundred warriors were sent here to Britannia and sta-tioned at Bremetennacum, to guard the western shore. When their twenty years of service were up, they settled here in the North and their sons entered the *Auxilla* after them. When the veterans were given citizenship, as the custom was, they took the family name of their commander, Artorius."

Ambros nodded. "Wasn't your grandmother named Arto-ria?"

"Just so. My cousin Argantel bears the name also, and keeps the Sword. It came to us through our great-grandmother, a druid's daughter who married the last of the Sarmatian soldier-priests who guarded it," Maderun went on. "It is an ancient blade, forged from star-steel by a magic that no smith in our day understands. In the hands of a great king, born of the ancient blood, it will bring victory."

"You are telling me that Vitalinus wants to be a great king, and would take the Sword?"

"He would," she said softly, "but he is not destined to wield it." She moved her mare up beside Ambros's hill pony. "A god lives in that Sword, who has promised that the Defender of Britannia will come of my cousin's blood. But the druid who must help him will come of mine."

Ambros's pony started to trot at the involuntary touch of his heels. He hauled back on the reins, abruptly making sense of a number of comments his mother had made in the past.

"And you think that *I* will be that Man of Wisdom?"

"I know that you are—" she said serenely. "And you must remember it when you go before this king."

Ambros felt his heart beat as if he had been running. "But what if I say the wrong thing?"

"Say what your heart tells you, and trust in God."

Which one? he wondered grimly. *The god of the Christians, or the one in the Sword, or whatever power my unknown father served?* He had been christened as a babe, but he thought sometimes that his alien blood had somehow repelled the Christian blessing. He attended mass with his mother, but he felt the mystery of the Spirit more strongly in the depths of the forest than he ever had within the chapel's walls.

Ambros grew very silent as the journey continued, for he had much to think about. Two days' travel brought them to the western coast. From there they rode northward, into the old Ordovici lands. Presently the way became more traveled. Boats were drawn up on the shore, and sacks and bales lay stacked under rude shelters.

They camped overnight by the water, and Ambros ran about talking to the sailors and workmen. If he was to grow up into a man of wisdom he would need to know about everything. And so he asked the sailors how they knew when a storm was coming, and the builders how they laid a foundation, and noted not only what they said but the pitying looks they thought he did not see.

Three more days of travel brought them to the Over-King.

Ambros sensed the hill almost before he saw it. A round summit, separate from the surrounding hills, it commanded the vale. The eastern face rose steeply, but their escort led them around to the southwest, where a path meandered slantwise across the slope. From here, one could see to the peak, where the trees had been felled to make way for the building. But there were no walls, only a great deal of tumbled stone.

The royal encampment sprawled over the meadows by the lake. A roundhouse had been erected to shelter the king; a gaggle of rudely thatched lesser buildings clustered around it, leaning a little drunkenly as if they had been built for a temporary use that had extended well beyond its term. The men were as motley as the dwellings.

Many were native British of types he recognized—horse-faced and redheaded Celts from the south or midlands, or the smaller, darker folk of the west. He saw men with the brown skins of legionary forebears from every corner of the Empire who spoke the British tongue with as pure an accent as any tribesman. But there were others, big, heavily muscled warriors with brown or ash-blond hair who exclaimed in deep-voiced gutturals. He knew these must be Saxons, hired mercenaries from across the sea.

A new language, Ambros thought with interest. He was quick at such things, and could read Latin from the church books almost as well as the priest already. He wondered how hard the Saxon tongue would be to learn.

Their escort brought them through the camp and drew up before the big roundhouse. Ambros felt his heart thumping heavily as he slid stiff-legged off his pony.

"The Vor-Tigernus is down by the lakeside," said the warrior who guarded the door. He was a big man called Hengest, the leader of the Saxon mercenaries. "He said you should take the boy to him when you came in."

Ambros was glad for the chance to walk some feeling back into his legs. He did not want them to think they were trembling because he was afraid. Still, as they made their way through the camp and down to the waterside he could not help holding very tightly to his mother's hand.

A group of older men stood on the lakeshore, watching another, who stood thigh deep in the water, holding a slender pole.

"He is fishing," said one of the men as Ambros looked up inquiringly, "we must keep still."

At home people generally used nets, which were more efficient both in time and results, but Ambros had sometimes caught fish in his hands, and knew how silent and attuned to the flow of the water one must be. The man who stood in the water did not move, but his mind was unquiet. And if Ambros could feel that, surely the fish would too. But maybe he did not care if he caught anything, so long as he could get away from other people for awhile.

Maderun was speaking in low tones to a tall man, richly dressed, with silver in his fair hair.

"This is Amlodius, your cousin by marriage. It seems a long time ago that we met—" She turned to the big man again. "Is Argantel well?"

"She is well in body. We had hopes of a child earlier this year, but it was not to be."

"That is always hard for a woman," Maderun sighed. "Take my love to her, when you return."

Amlodius started to reply, then stilled. The fisherman was coming in. The skin on his head was sunburnt beneath the thinning ginger hair, and the skirts of his tunic flapped wetly around his legs, but no one laughed. Instead of the kind of majesty Ambros had expected, he moved with a driving purpose that was in its own way just as compelling. A slave brought up a stool for him to sit on and took his fishing pole. Ambros stiffened as the Over-King's gaze swept the little group and fixed upon him.

"This is the boy, sir," said one of the messengers. Vitalinus beckoned him forward.

"Do you know why you were brought here?" His voice was an even tenor, neither warm nor cold.

"You are building a fortress and it keeps falling down. Your wise men said I could help you, and you will reward my family if I do—" Ambros shrugged and glanced at the two men in the multi-checkered mantles of druids who stood nearby.

"Perhaps, if you are the right boy," said Vitalinus. "Lady Maderun, I understand this is your son. You must tell me truthfully how he was begotten."

Maderun came forward to stand beside Ambros and he took her hand.

"I can say this, my lord, and may God be my witness. Until I was married, after this boy's birth, I never lay with a man. They will have told you that on my journey home from my cousin's wedding I was lost for a time in the forest. What happened to me there I do not remember, but my son was born a full twelve-month afterward, so I do not think he was gotten then. When I lay recovering in the convent I dreamed often of a man as fair as the dawn who came to me. Be he angel or demon I do not know, but that he was my child's father I believe, and no earthly man."

Ambros looked up at his mother with interest. *Does she have an invisible friend too*?

"Maugantius, is this possible?" The king turned to his house-priest, who was looking thoughtful.

"As you know, I have studied the writings of the Romans as well as the Church fathers," he said at last. "And it may be so. In *De Deo Socratis*, Apuleus tells us of beings that live between the earth and the moon which have partly the nature of men and partly that of angels. The ancients called them *daimons*, but we know that they are *incubi*, or *succubi* if they come in female form. It is said that they delight in tempting mortals to impurity. Perhaps one of these appeared to this woman and begot the lad."

"He does not look like the son of an angel," said Vitalinus

thoughtfully. "But he does seem to fulfill the terms of the prophecy. My druids have told me that the blood of a fatherless boy is needed to bless the foundations of my fortress. What have you to say to that, Ambros who is no man's son?" he said suddenly.

Maderun gasped and gripped his shoulders protectively.

They did not tell my mother why they wanted me, but I think they told Morobrin! Ambros felt terror shock through him and then drain away, leaving him very still. Neither of the two druids would meet his gaze.

"They are fools," said a still, sweet voice in his head. "*Go to the hilltop and the spirits in the earth will tell you what is wrong.*"

"I think that they are stupid," he said in a voice he did not recognize. "You need me with my blood in my veins, not on the ground. The earth speaks to me. Take me to the top of your hill, and I will tell you what she says." Saying the words opened his awareness to the voices in the wind and water. He could feel the flow of energy beneath his feet as he did sometimes in the forest at home.

"It is true that death is very final," said the Vor-Tigernus. "But you must understand that this fortress is an essential link in the chain of strongholds I am building to defend this land. I will do whatever is needful to establish it."

Ambros met the Over-King's eyes and saw something, perhaps a spark of recognition, kindle in that amber gaze. "You act from need . . ." he said, "but I, from necessity. . . ."

Ambros felt as if he was two people, the one who was climbing the hill, answering questions as if he were a spirit himself, and the other, who was only a little boy, and afraid. But there was a third within him, and it was she who comforted the one who feared and counseled the one who climbed. Perhaps, he thought, she was a *daimon* like the one who had come to his mother. It was a long climb, but Ambros noted with some satisfaction that the adults tired before he did.

Except for the Over-King. Agile as a fox, Vitalinus mounted

the path ahead of him, and when they arrived at the summit he was not even winded.

"Behold Britannia spread out before you," said the Vor-Tigernus. "Is it not a fair prospect?" Below them the lake shone bright as blue enamelwork in the sun, surrounded by folded green hills.

"Is that why you want to build a fortress here?"

"I will be remembered. I will defend this land!"

Ambros looked at him, and echoing the voice within, replied, "It is true. You will be remembered."

Vitalinus, sensing something sardonic in the boy's tone, turned to him with narrowed eyes. "And what do you say now that you are here? Your life hangs on it, boy, so speak to me."

At the center of the summit was a hollow, where coarse marsh grasses grew. Ambros made his way to the center, squatted down, and laid his two palms against the ground. With his eyes closed his hearing sharpened, and it seemed to him he could hear running water. His awareness expanded, and he felt two streams of energy, one coming all the way from the farthest point on the holy isle of Mona to the northwest and the other from the Isle of the Dead to the southwest, winding through the earth like serpents to cross beneath the peak.

"The Dragon Path . . ." he whispered, looking up at the king. "You are building on the Dragon Path. Why have your druids not told you?" Once more he sent his awareness downward where the forces churned uneasily, disturbed by the digging.

"*Tell the Vor-Tigernus he must dig down until he reaches the water—*" came his inner voice. Ambros did not realize he had repeated the words aloud until Vitalinus began to shout for his builders.

"Your head is not safe yet, boy," he said as men ran off to do his bidding, "but if you are right about this I will begin to believe."

For the rest of that day and the next every man who could hold a shovel was set to digging, stopping only when darkness fell. Ambros and his mother were treated well, but they were carefully guarded. The boy slept fitfully, dreaming of warring dragons.

On the third day the mud the workmen had been digging gave way to a bubbling spring, which rapidly washed away the remaining earth around it until they were looking down at a clear pool.

"Your druids could not even tell you what was underneath the ground," said Ambros. "They were wrong about me as well."

"Perhaps. But I still must make the foundations for my fortress."

Ambros eyed him uncertainly, but the Over-King was smiling. A little wind ruffled the surface of the water; or was it something from below? The boy looked upward and saw clouds moving in from the northwest, but the disturbance he felt came from somewhere deep in the hill.

The two druids watched him, muttering, and he turned to them.

"If you are so wise, tell the king what is underneath the pool!"

"Earth and stone are underneath the water," said one, but the other kept silent.

"And what do you say is underneath the pool, oh fatherless child?" asked the Vor-Tigernus.

"Dragons . . ." whispered Ambros. "I would tell you to leave this place, but you will not do it. Command your men to drain this pool, and you will see."

Once more the laborers were summoned. Working with pick and drill, they made a channel through the side of the hill. As the work proceeded the wind grew stronger, blowing now from one direction and now from the other. Overhead, clouds were gathering. Light from the westering sun slanted golden beneath them, gilding the metal of the shovels and turning the grass a vivid green.

Ambros sat on the ground, frowning beneath his heavy brows. He could hear men marveling at how swiftly the wind was driving the storm, but he knew it was not the wind, but an echo of the disturbance in the hill. As the level of the channel neared that of the pool, he got up and edged backward. When he approached the oak trees that grew at the rim of the hill, two warriors barred his way.

"Very well, I will stay—" He sat down again. "But take my mother a little ways down the hill. Tell her it is because of the storm."

The man's grim expression softened a little and he turned to do as Ambros had asked. Vitalinus had been eyeing them suspiciously, but when the boy sat down he resumed his watch on the pool. The last cut was made, well below the level of the pool, and the water began to sink rapidly, swirling in a widdershins vortex toward the hidden hole. So swiftly did it spin that a fine spray flew up from it, continuing to whirl in the wind. In another moment it seemed as if the clouds themselves had caught the motion. Wind whipped at men's mantles and blew anything lightweight away.

Ambros hunkered down where he was, fingers digging into the grass. Leaning against the wind, Vitalinus stumbled toward him.

"What is it?" he cried, staring up at the storm. "What is happening?"

Ambros looked up at the clouds shot with lightnings, partly a dirty white, and partly tinged red by the setting sun. Then his focus changed and he allowed himself to see the energies that other senses had shown him.

"The Dragons are fighting!" Ambros shouted back, waving upward. "The Red Dragon, and the White!" Storm-white and crimson, the sinuous forms roiled; now the white one taking the ascendant and then the other claiming victory. "Don't you see them? Can't you *see*?" He gripped the Vor-Tigernus's shoulder and felt the man stiffen and knew that at least for that moment he *did* see.

The White Dragon had risen from the path that came up from the southeast toward Mona; the Crimson from the line of power that crossed it. The earth trembled with the force of their conflict. But gradually, as he watched he could see that the

White Dragon was forcing its opponent downward. Lightning flared, and in the next instant they were deafened by a clap of thunder. Blinking, Ambros saw the Crimson Dragon sink into the earth and disappear. But the White circled upward on the storm, spiraled three times widdershins around the hill, then sped away in the direction it had come.

The great wind died away as suddenly as it had appeared, and the hilltop stood silent. The last light of the sun picked out the wreckage strewn across the grass and the empty hole in the ground. Men picked themselves up, staring about them. One by one, they gathered around the Vor-Tigernus and the boy.

"What does it mean? Why did they come?" Vitalinus picked Ambros up and stood him on his feet. The boy rubbed his eyes. He felt dizzy, and his vision was still seared by that last lightning flash, so that he saw in shadows speckled with little sparks of light.

He started to say that he did not know, but in his head his invisible friend was speaking. As he listened he began to weep, because he was very tired, and what she was saying filled him with fear. He shook his head, but the terrible knowledge would not go away, and in the end, it was easier to close his eyes and let her use his voice to say the words.

"The Red Dragon belongs to the tribes. It is part of this land."

"And the White?" The question seemed to come from a long ways away.

"The White comes from over the sea. It follows the path of the conquerors, the way the first Romans came. The White Dragon belongs to the Saxon folk that you have called into this land. In blood and fire they will rise against you, and only in these mountains will the Red Dragon find refuge from the foe. . . ."

With the words came images: burning cities, dead children lying sprawled like abandoned dolls, fleeing families pursued by fair-haired men with bloody swords. It was too much for him—consciousness fled inward, while from his lips the dreadful prophecies rolled on and on.

When Ambros awakened he knew it had been a long time because it was dark. Beside the empty pool a bonfire was blazing. He lay with his head in his mother's lap, wrapped warmly. He felt empty, as if only his mother's touch anchored him to earth. He stirred a little, and one of the people who had been watching over him ran off. Presently a shadow came between him and the fire, and he looked up and saw the Over-King.

"So, Ambros, you have confounded my men of wisdom," said Vitalinus.

"They were fools. . . . Will you give my mother the gold?" Ambros swallowed. His voice was hoarse, as if he had been shouting. Maderun offered him some warmed milk in a panniken and he drank it gratefully.

"I will keep my word," said the king. "But if my druids are fools I must send them away. Stay with me, Ambros, and be my prophet."

"But he is only a boy!" exclaimed Maderun.

"Is he?" Their gazes locked above Ambros's head.

If I go home, thought Ambros, *Dinabu will tease me and my stepfather will glower and wish me gone. Here, where so many men come and go, maybe I can find out who I am. . . .*

"I will stay," the boy said into the tense silence, and Vitalinus turned back to look at him. Ambros gazed up into those yellow eyes, and in the end, it was the Vor-Tigernus of Britannia who looked away.

THE FORGE

A.D. 437

T HE WISE MEN OF BRITANNIA WERE DEBATING IN THE OVER-KING'S
hall. In the portico of what had once been the palace of the
Roman governor of Britannia, the philosopher and priest Maugantius, who studied the stars; a druid from the lands of the
Votadini called Maglicun and another from Guenet named
Melerius; and Godwulf, the Saxon thyle, argued beneath the
dispassionate gaze of painted gods. With them sat Father Felix,
who had been a student of Pelagius, and Martinus, come over
from Gaul to preach the new theology by which Augustinus
of Hippo explained the disasters that had overtaken the empire. And just beyond the circle of light cast by the brazier, the
king's prophet, Ambros son of Maderun, sat listening, with his
back against a marble pillar and his arms around his knees.

Some of the Vor-Tigernus's wise men viewed Ambros as a
mindless vehicle for prophecy. Such creatures were born from
time to time—unable to speak properly or care for themselves,
but capable of great feats of calculation, or of repeating back
lists of names and lore. But Ambros was something else, a wild
child with an endless thirst for knowledge. Remembering his
mother's teaching, he kept quiet and made himself useful, and
they condescended to let him listen to their discussions, though
they did not suspect how much he had learned.

At eleven, he had the growth of a boy of fourteen, all long legs and clumsy feet with a head that seemed too large for his body and teeth too big for his jaws. It had been some time since Vitalinus had called on him for prophecy. *Maybe*, thought Ambros as he listened to the men's voices, *when I grow up the gift will leave me, and I will be an ordinary man.*

"It does not matter how hard you strive," said the new priest, Martinus. "You will still fall so short of God's perfection that only His grace can save you, as He has predestined."

Ambros did not yet know what Martinus might have to teach him, for the Gaulish priest still crossed himself and muttered charms against the devil when the boy came too near. Now, he saw Ambros watching him and his fiery gaze flinched away.

"And I call that a heresy!" exclaimed Felix. "I believe in a God of justice, who will reward good works done in His name. Will you tell our lord that all his labor to protect this land meant nothing? For twelve years the wolves have been kept from our borders, and Britannia has prospered as never before."

Felix was a priest in the civilized tradition of the later empire, able to argue philosophy as well as theology, viewing other faiths with an easy tolerance so long as they prayed for Britannia. He had taught Ambros to work hard and to value the wonderful variety of humankind. The boy smiled as Felix continued, for he had heard all this before.

"The Vor-Tigernus has pacified the men of Eriu by marrying his daughter to their king, and the Irish who remained in Guenet are being cast out by the Votadini. Those who tried to take Dumnonia were defeated by the Cornovii whom he has settled there. Coelius and the Army defend the lands around Eburacum, and Amlodius those of Luguvalium, and our allies in Dun Breatann and Dun Eidyn are a further bulwark against the painted people of the North. In the South and East we are protected from the Saxon wolves who formerly savaged these shores by Hengest and his men! All these forces are commanded by the Vor-Tigernus!"

"Praise ice when you have crossed over it, and a king when he is on the funeral pyre..." rumbled Godwulf. "Hengest guards you now, but he cannot do so if Vitalinus does not pay his men."

"Let the men of the South and East who have grown rich in these times of peace pay them!" exclaimed Maglicun. "The north must support its own defenders."

It had taken some time for the druids' suspicions of Ambros to ease, but in the end they had remembered his mother's connection to the Isle of Maidens and accepted the boy. Perhaps the alacrity with which he learned from the other sages had something to do with it also, for as Maglicun said, it was not fitting that a child of the ancient priestly line of Britannia should grow up knowing nothing of his true heritage.

"I do not think they will," Father Felix said unhappily. "They complain about the Vor-Tigernus's taxes and talk of calling the sons of Ambrosius Augustus back from Armorica to rule them."

"It is not Justice that Vitalinus needs, but Mercy," put in Martinus. "If all his labors are in vain, will not that prove the truth of Bishop Augustinus's teaching?"

"The stars show that a time of changes is coming, but whether for good or ill I do not know." Maugantius pulled at his beard thoughtfully.

Ambros had found Maugantius more approachable than most of the others, and through many long nights had kept him company as the philosopher watched the constellations wheel across the sky. Maugantius was a follower of Plato and his later disciples, Iamblichus and Porphyry, an initiate of Greek mysteries and Egyptian magic dedicated to the Great Work by which a man might re-forge himself into a god.

Maglicun snorted. "Of course there will be changes. Night gives birth to day and winter to spring. It is the way of the world to turn in a circle, not in a straight line as you Christians say. The end of one thing is the beginning of another. The wise man learns to interpret these cycles, and moves with them rather than fighting the flow."

Ambros nodded. This was the wisdom of his mother's people, and it nourished something in his soul. But all this talk of change was making him uneasy. Would Vitalinus ask him to prophesy? Could he still do it? At the thought, he felt the familiar wave of dizziness and the presence of his invisible friend, awakening suddenly in his mind like an old tune.

He shook his head and pinched himself to reconnect with his body. *No! I don't want to see what is coming! I don't want to know.*

"That is so," Godwulf was saying, "but the little priest says truly that those threads the Norns have spun may not be broken. In the end, it is not the outcome that matters, but the way a man meets his wyrd. Still, one may face what is to be all the better for some warning. I will cast the runes and see what they say."

From the thyle, Ambros had learned some of the runelore of the Eruli, and found it powerful but strange. Godwulf turned, as if he had felt Ambros staring at him, and the boy felt that premonitory dizziness brush his mind once more.

"We must speak to the men on the Council, and to the Over-King," Melerius said then. "We must make them understand."

These were wise men, thought Ambros, and they would speak with wisdom. But in the end he knew that the Vor-Tigernus would call on the wild power that spoke through the boy without a father, and Ambros could not predict what that power might say.

The river Ictis meandered gently through reedbed and meadow, its quiet belying the proximity of Venta Belgarum, whose tiled roofs could just be glimpsed beyond the trees. The spring had been wet, and the water ran high and strong, but its surface was calm, veiling its power. With the warmer days of summer, vegetation had grown lushly green, at times almost blocking the path beside the stream. But Ambros pushed determinedly onward, looking over his shoulder from time to time at the roof of the basilica where the Vor-Tigernus sat in Council with the lords of Britannia. He was well out of earshot, but it seemed to him that the sound of angry voices still echoed inside his skull.

The day had the sultry stillness that heralded a storm, though there was no cloud in the sky. He paused, looking down into the brown waters, his sharp eyes catching the sinuous movement of the speckled bass and silver-scaled bream, but although he might for a moment touch the slow, quiet thoughts of the fish that hid in those depths he could not forget the passions of humankind. Maugantius had tried to teach him the skill by which a man can barrier his soul from the emotions of others, but Ambros had not yet mastered it. He wondered if even Maugantius had the power to shut out awareness of what was happening today.

For three days they had been arguing, Vitalinus insisting that the rich landowners of the Midlands and the West should contribute to the defense of their eastern neighbors. And for three days the magnates of Britannia had countered that the danger from which the mercenaries had been hired to protect them was past, and it was foolishness to maintain an army when there was no enemy. And throughout it all Hengest, Vitalinus's *magister militum*, stood at his master's right hand and said nothing at all.

Ambros turned his back on the city and kept walking. From above, the musical "ke-ar" of a hawk came drifting down on the wind. He peered upward, shading his eyes with one hand, and glimpsed a tiny speck against the blue. From such a height the doings of men must seem without significance, he told himself. And yet the hawk's sharp eyes caught the tiniest movements of the small scurrying creatures that moved through the grass. *Is that how the gods see us?* he wondered. It was an uncomfortable thought, and he moved on.

Presently, over the gentle murmur of the stream he heard a musical "tink, tink." In another moment a shift in the wind brought him the scent of charcoal and scorched metal, and he knew he was nearing a forge.

The noise grew louder. Ambros saw a path leading away from the river and followed it. Beneath an ancient oak tree

stood an unhitched wagon. Nearby, the cart-horse was cropping the grass, while the smith, barrel-chested and bandy-
legged, with arms like gnarled trees, hammered at a horseshoe
for a dappled mare. He was a freedman, Ambros saw from the
Phrygian cap he wore; probably one of those who traveled
from farm to villa, plying his trade. Two more horses awaited
his attention, tied to trees.

As Ambros neared, the smith finished hammering, took the
shoe from the anvil and lifted the horse's hoof to try it, then
swore softly and laid it back on the coals of the forge. As he
did so, he saw Ambros watching.

"You, boy—come give me a hand with the bellows. You
look strong, and my own lad's run off to gawk at the great
ones in the town."

Amused, for even the Vor-Tigernus did not order him about
in quite so peremptory a tone, Ambros set his hand to the work
and quickly got the knack of it.

"Fire's like a man, you see," said the smith, "that will die if
you don't give him air."

"And the iron?" asked Ambros.

"Ah, that's like a man too, a strong man who's hardened
and shaped by the blows life deals him. But sometimes you'll
find a piece of metal, or a man, with a hidden flaw. You strike
him wrong and he'll shatter." The horseshoe glowed a dull red
when he plucked it from the fire, but the color faded quickly
as he began to hammer it once more.

"Are the best pieces the purest?" asked Ambros as the smith
got the horse's leg between his knees and set the shoe against
the hoof once more. The metal was still hot enough to singe,
and the boy wrinkled his nose at the scent of hot horn. This
time the shoe fit, and the smith changed hammers and began
to nail it down with swift, precise taps.

"Not always." He let go and the horse stamped, unused to
the weight of the shoe. "For some things, like swords, you
want to melt a little of something else, nickel, for instance, into
the iron. If you forge rods whose metal is different together,

the sword has the strength of all of them, not just one. Do you understand?"

Ambros nodded, and the smith took up another shoe blank and laid it on the fire. The boy had sometimes watched the smiths who traveled with the Vor-Tigernus, but his ambiguous position in the court constrained communication. To this man, he was only a boy. Ambros applied himself to the bellows once more, watching with satisfaction as the coals began to pulse and glow.

"You work well," said the smith. "Have your people set you to a trade?"

"I'm only eleven."

"That's not too soon to begin, if you're strong. What do your folk mean you to be?"

A Man of Wisdom, thought Ambros, but that was his mother's saying, not his own. And there were many kinds of wisdom.

"I don't know what metal I'm made of . . ." he answered, "or who's to have the forging of me." A flock of rooks flew overhead, calling raucously; he looked up to follow their flight and saw the sun disappearing behind the trees. He let go of the bellows and straightened. The work had freed him from his worries for most of the afternoon.

"I have to go. I'm sorry—" he added, "I liked helping you."

"Did you?" The smith's laughter echoed from the trees and the horses tossed their heads nervously. "Do not grieve then, for we will meet again, and when we do, perhaps you will know what you are."

Ambros's steps dragged as he headed homeward, watching the white swans sail the quiet stream. But as he neared the bridge the echo of the smith's laughter was drowned out by a great clamor from the town. He stopped, staring, as riders clattered over the bridge and set their mounts at a gallop down the road—they belonged to Gerontius of Dumnonia, by the emblem. A few moments later they were followed by a horse-litter surrounded by guards. That was Sulpicius from Deva. What was going on?

He crossed the bridge between cavalcades and tugged at a shopkeeper's sleeve.

"Vitalinus has dismissed the Council!" came the answer. "Or they've dismissed him, it's hard to say. But the great ones are off to their own lands, and talk goes that they've sworn to bring Ambrosius Aurelianus and his brother back from Armorica to be our emperors!"

Vitalinus moved swiftly, marshalling the forces that were left to him. But with the warriors of Dumnonia and Guenet turned against him, and Coelius protesting that the Painted Peoples would attack if he weakened the Army of the North, they were few. Even Amlodius, protesting that after so many years of marriage his wife was about to give birth to a living child at last, refused to come, though he sent a subcommander with some of his men.

From his own lands around Glevum the Vor-Tigernus had the men he had trained, and some from the south coast, but for the most part his strength lay in the barbarian troops who for the past ten seasons had guarded the land. And where they had come from there were many more.

While the sons of Ambrosius gathered forces in the west country, Hengest sent swift ships across the channel to bring more warriors from the German lands. While he waited for them to arrive the Over-King evaded Aurelianus's attempts to bring him to battle, knowing that if he could delay long enough, many of the rebels would go home to help get the harvest in.

The two forces came together at last just before the festival of Lugos at a place called Uollopum, north of Venta Belgarum. Not all of the Vor-Tigernus's reinforcements had arrived, but Aurelianus forced the issue, for he was beginning to lose men. Through all one bloody day they struggled, while Ambros and the other noncombatants watched from a hill nearby. And because their numbers were almost even, when darkness fell neither side could claim the victory. The Ambrosian forces withdrew to Dumnonia to lick their wounds, and Vitalinus and his men fell back toward Glevum.

The sword flares down, slicing through leather armor, cleaving flesh and bone. A man screams as his arm is torn from his body; then blood sprays crimson and the voice is stilled. Others fill the silence, crying out in pain or rage. The clangor of weapons assaults the senses. The smell of blood and sweat and shit fouls the air.

He whimpers, trying to find a way out of the carnage, but everywhere he turns he finds faces contorted in rage, and the swift flare of bloodied swords. . . . He curls in a ball, trying to get away, away. . . .

"Ambros!"

He flinched as a hand gripped his shoulder and jerked upright on the bench, flailing. The fingers let go and someone laughed. Ambros blinked, saw Hengest looming over him and behind the Saxon, Vitalinus.

"Wake up, boy. Your master needs music to sweeten his mood!" The Saxon laughed again and turned away.

Ambros rubbed his eyes. The only fighting he could see was the battle between the Greeks and the centaurs painted on the wall of the villa where they had stopped for the night, and the angry voice he heard belonged to the Vor-Tigernus.

A slave scurried in with a pitcher of spiced wine. Vitalinus took it before the slave could set it down and refilled his cup, drank deeply, coughed, and drank again.

"Emperor! He dares to take the purple on the strength of one battle which he did not win!" Vitalinus glared around the room.

As his senses returned, Ambros remembered the messenger who had ridden in just before suppertime. That was what had sent the great ones to council. From the sound of it, nothing had been resolved.

"Neither did you," Hengest said drily. "Nor will you, unless you get more men." Despite the guttural accent, he spoke Latin fluently and could make himself understood in the British tongue. He stood with his back to the fire, his face hidden, but his shadow stretched dark across the room.

The Vor-Tigernus poured more wine and began to pace up and down. As he passed Ambros he paused.

"You heard him, child. Take up your harp and see if music will soothe the savage heart of your king!"

Eyeing his master warily, Ambros reached for the harp, a simple crescent of oakwood joined to a soundbox, with five horsehair strings.

"Go on—or do you think yourself a David to my Saul? I will not throw a lance at you!" He jerked into motion once more, slopping wine upon the floor.

No, Ambros thought, *I am not David, for I will never be a king. . . .*

He settled the harp against his shoulder. He had learned to play simple chords and accompany the bards when they chanted the old songs, but he did not think that singing was wanted just now. Softly he began to pluck the thirds and fifths of harmony.

Perhaps the sound did have a soothing effect, for he saw Vitalinus's high color recede and presently the king sat down. He looked at his *magister militum* and sighed.

"You are right. I need more men. Can you conjure them out of the air?"

"Out of the air?" Hengest's deep laughter rumbled in his chest. "That I cannot do. But I can bring them out of the water—over the sea—"

There was a long silence. Ambros clutched the harp, scarcely daring to touch the strings.

"I know. In your country there are many warriors. But they will not fight for love of me," Vitalinus said at last. "If I had the gold to pay them—to pay *you*—I would not be sitting here now."

Hengest sat down before the hearth, clasping his knees. Sitting so, his head was still as high as the king's shoulder, but he no longer loomed over him.

"When I give the gold you pay me to my men, they send it

home so that their kindred can buy food that their sea-soaked land will no longer bear. If you have no gold, you possess what my people hold dearer—black earth from which grows the golden corn."

The Vor-Tigernus started, staring down at the other man, but he made no sound. After a moment the soft rumble of Hengest's voice resumed.

"Hirelings must be paid, but there is no question of payment between allies. Give us land, Lord of Britannia, as the emperors of Rome gave Germania Prima to the Burgunds, and Aquitanica to the Visigoths. As guest with host we shall dwell, and take our living from the produce of the land."

"As *feoderati*—" said Vitalinus.

"As allies," repeated Hengest. "And to seal the bargain I will give you a hostage from my own family. You have seen my daughter—"

She had come over from Germania just this year, Ambros remembered, a tall woman, with red-gold hair, and beautiful.

"Reginwynna . . ." breathed Vitalinus.

"You have no woman. Take Reginwynna as your wife, and give us Cantium."

"It cannot work!" Vitalinus jerked out of his chair and began to pace about the room. "The lords of Britannia will never stand for it."

"It has worked for the Romans," Hengest objected. "Are you not the emperor?"

Vitalinus shrugged. "My fathers were magistrates under Rome, but I do not come of the old princely lines. Aurelianus is kin to the old kings of Demetia and Guenet. If I had something—some symbol of sovereignty that might command men's allegiance, I could rule as I willed." For a long moment he stared into the fire. Then he turned.

Ambros felt the hairs rise on the back of his neck as he realized that the Vor-Tigernus was looking at *him*.

"Your mother comes of the old blood of the North, is it not so? I have heard tales of a Sword. . . ."

Ambros was shaking his head, but he could feel the pressure of Vitalinus's will like a fire.

"Put down your harp, son of Maderun, and speak to me words of truth and prophecy—" the Vor-Tigernus's words sparked through his awareness.

I cannot. . . . I will not. . . . I swore not to speak of the Sword! thought Ambros, but already his vision was blurring. His will was a fraying tether, and his consciousness a wild thing eager to break free.

"In the name of God and his holy angels I command you, and in the name of the Old Powers of this land. Four winters I have fed and clothed you, and I am your lord."

He was a king, and accustomed to be obeyed. Against the authority in that tone Ambros had no defenses. Desperate, he sought his inner *daimon*, and as the inrush of her presence released him from himself, faintly he heard a voice that was not quite his own begin to answer the king.

"Woe to the lord who summons powers he cannot command!" An eerie, tinkling laughter made Vitalinus step back. "You have asked, oh King, but can you understand the answer? I see the White Dragon growing strong; his children flourish in the land. The Red Dragon rises to fight against them, and blood covers the ground. The children of the Red Dragon are slain."

"And what of the Sword?" As from a great distance, he heard the Vor-Tigernus ask.

"The Boar of Dumnonia rages and the White Dragon is brought to bay; but he in turn shall be brought low and his brother shall rule. But the Sword of the God of War is not for him, for he shall be slain. After him shall come the young bear, begotten by a man who is dead upon a secret queen. No man but he may draw the Sword from the Stone."

"And what of me? How shall I save this land?"

"You have sown the teeth of the dragon and you must reap the harvest. . . ."

The voice came to Ambros like a whisper on the wind. His

body was falling, but his spirit fell further, descending forever down a tunnel of night until he knew no more.

Ambros opened his eyes to darkness. He lay on the bench, and someone had covered him with a cloak, but he was alone in the room. He sat up, rubbing his forehead to relieve the dull ache behind his eyes, and pulled the wool around him. A dim glow from the hearth enabled him to make out his surroundings; from somewhere nearby came a faint snoring.

What had the daimon that lived within him said to the king? Nothing good, for he could remember someone shouting. If he was still alive and free it must be because the king thought him too weakened by his trance to be worth guarding. But tomorrow the Vor-Tigernus would certainly punish him.

At the thought, volition came back to his limbs. Ambros wrapped the cloak around him, took a partly eaten loaf of bread from the Vor-Tigernus's plate and stuffed it down the front of his tunic, and poked his head out the door.

He heard snores and harsh breathing, but nothing stirred.

The gods of his people must be protecting him, thought Ambros as he passed through the gate of the villa, for the one guard he had seen had been sleeping. A waning moon showed him his way, and soon he was on the Londinium road. No one would expect him to flee that way, but from there he could double around to the north and then head west to Demetia.

Though the road was not so well maintained as it had been under the Romans, Ambros made good time, and by dawn he was approaching the White Horse Vale. He paused, gazing southward in wonder, as the first light revealed first the noble curve of the downs against the eastern sky, and then, as the sun rose, the attenuated curves of white that revealed the Horse shape carved into the chalk of the hills.

Ambros's breath caught. He remembered suddenly the sculptured curves of bone in the skull of the White Mare that led the procession at Samhain. Swathed in a white horsehide, the Mare was at once the face of Death and the promise of life to come, for she brought the spirits of the ancestors in her train to take flesh once more in the wombs of the women of the tribe. The blood of his mother's people beat in his temples as he gazed upon that mighty form, bound into the very bones of the land.

"White Mare, protect me—" he whispered, then glanced behind him. There was nothing there now, but soon, folk would be stirring, and might remember a strange lad hurrying down the road. But if he struck out across country here, he should strike the Ridgeway, that ancient trail that followed the top of the downs east and north. From there he could spot any pursuers long before he could be seen.

The Vale was bigger than it had looked in the deceptive light of dawn. All that day, the boy struggled to cross it, detouring around meadows whose green hid marshland still soggy from the spring rains. Farm roads petered out in woodlots or pastures, and sometimes he had to hide from men working in the fields. Thus, by the time he began the long climb up to the Ridgeway, dusk was drawing a veil of shadow across the land.

Ambros found the ancient track more by touch than by eyesight, stumbling even when he reached the summit and the smoother ground. He flinched from a flicker of motion, then saw it was a hunting owl, gliding by on noiseless wings. With nightfall, the downs became a different country. He was acutely aware of the mighty swell of the chalk, as if the bones of the earth were pushing through the soil. And the longer he followed the Ridgeway, the more conscious he became of the many feet that had trod that path before.

This was an ancient land, where any stone might be an elf-bolt lost before the fathers of the British tribes ever came over the sea. Some said that the little dark hunters, or their spirits, wandered here still. Ambros glanced over his shoulder, wondering if they hunted by night or by day. The open expanse that had attracted him in the morning seemed now to impose a terrible vulnerability. Uplifted on the shoulders of the downs, he cowered beneath the huge expanse of sky, seeking, like some small scurrying animal benighted far from its burrow, a place to hide.

And so, when he saw a stand of beech trees in dark silhouette against the southern sky, he turned off the path.

Almost at once an odd scent stopped him. Ambros sniffed cautiously, and his nostrils flared at the harsh reek of a charcoal fire. He took a step forward, fancying he saw the glow of flames behind the trees, and then, unmistakably, came the chink of metal on metal, and he recognized the music of the forge.

"Come warm yourself—" a deep voice called him forth from among the beeches. "I have stew to fill your belly as well."

Amazement warred with caution, for this was the same man Ambros had met beside the river at Venta Belgarum. But more powerful still was hunger, for beside the bread he had eaten nothing that day. Licking his lips, he stepped into the light of the blacksmith's fire.

The flickering flames showed him the horse and wagon, and behind them a tumble of stone like a fallen wall. But four mighty uprights still stood among them, flanking a dark passage that led into the mound.

"What are you doing here?" He heard his own voice, stupid with fatigue.

"Shoeing horses—what else?" The smith grinned. "In this country there are many fine ones. The people will bring them to me when they gather in the old fortress for the fair."

There is a fine white mare on the hillside, thought Ambros. *Will you set shoes on Her as well?*

But more important than fear or fancy was hunger, and he dug into the bowl of stewed pork which the smith handed him. There was ale as well, stronger than he was used to, with an aftertaste of honey. The smith continued to tap away with his hammer, talking of the the fair with its horse races and peddlers from many lands, when the people scoured away the grass that encroached around the edges of the Horse's limbs. Ambros could not quite see what he was making, and after a time his eyes grew heavy and he forgot to look.

The chink of the hammer came regular as a pulsebeat, but as Ambros began to drowse, it seemed to him that what the smith was beating out was not metal but memories, a sequence of bright images that passed before him until he walked among them. The dark hunters of the hills chipped skillfully at the flint to make their arrowheads and axes. They were followed by a bigger, brown-haired folk who tilled the land and dragged great stones from the mountains to entomb their dead, using hand axes to peck cups and spirals into the rock. Ambros saw the first mound made beneath the beech trees, and then the building of the barrow of stones.

He was sitting in a place of ghosts, he thought dimly, but he sensed a circle of safety in the light of the blacksmith's fire. In dream he saw the leaves of countless seasons drift down across the stones. A new tribe came who drank their ale from beakers of fired clay banded with patterns made by cord or comb, and after them people whose smiths crafted fine weapons of polished bronze, who brought more stones to set in careful alignments where the dragon power flowed through the land. Circles of shaped stone marked the movements of sun and moon with more precision than any of Maugantius's formulae. The makers of the old tombs were forgotten, and bronze-smiths plied their craft before the mound.

And yet these tribes also passed into memory. The weather grew colder, with more rain, and the upland farms were abandoned. Men used new and better weapons of bronze to fight for what arable land remained, and built earth-walled fortresses to defend their territory. Ambros did not understand all that he saw, but he could see a pattern, in which one people succeeded another in lordship of the land.

And presently there came tall, bright-haired folk from across the sea who carried swords of iron, and worked their ornaments in sinuous spirals varied with palmettes and scrolls. He knew them for British, his mother's people, but in his dream they seemed no more than another layering of leaves on the mound. The click of stone axe on stone became the ring of bronze, and then the heavy clangor of iron as, generation after generation, the smiths worked their magic, compelling the inert elements of earth to the service of man.

His head throbbed to the ring of those hammers until he could no longer see, and then it seemed to Ambros that he himself was lifted and laid upon the anvil. The hammer swung, shattering his old form and shaping him anew. He understood at last what the atoms of which the old Greek magi had written must be, for he could feel each atom in his body realigning beneath the blows. And as he looked up, he saw that somehow the gnarled blacksmith had become a radiant goddess, with hair of flame.

"You were a raw lump, but I have made of you a mighty weapon for the hand of the destined king. But let the lord who makes use of you remember that truth is a two-edged sword. . . ."

Then he was taken from the anvil and sheathed in something soft and warm, and sank into a sleep of darkness too deep for dreams.

Ambros woke slowly. He ached as if he had been beaten all over, but at least he was warm. One eye opened, and then the other. He lay wrapped in the cloak on a bed of sweet-smelling grasses, but above and to either side of him he saw stone. With a shiver he realized that he was lying inside the mound. Still, the light had to be coming from somewhere. Wincing, he turned over, and saw at the end of the passageway a pale square of sky. He caught a whiff of woodsmoke and then the scent of meat, and his stomach rumbled.

After a struggle, he freed himself from the cloak and crawled toward the daylight.

There was the fire, as he remembered. But there was no wagon, only a muddy horse cropping the grass. Blinking, he peered at the man who sat toasting strips of venison over the flames. The broad shoulders were familiar, but they did not belong to the smith. It was Hengest who was sitting there.

The Saxon lifted a strip of meat and handed the end of the skewer to Ambros. It was hot, but perhaps his encounter with the smith had been a dream, for he was furiously hungry.

"How did you find me?" he asked when he had finished the first piece and was working on a second one.

"I followed the White Horse," came the reply. "For my people, the white stallion is holy. The way he runs tells the priests what is to be. Sometimes when a tribe must move, they loose the stallion, and where he goes they follow. You also see the future—I knew he would lead me to you."

"Did the Vor-Tigernus send you after me?"

"My lord is not happy—" Beneath the grizzled mustache Hengest's lips twitched. "But in this he does not command me." His blue gaze fixed the boy. "Our wise men teach that Woden, who gives the ecstasy that carries men to victory in battle, gives also staves of verse to the shope, and the spirit speech of the *witega*, the wise-man. I think that you belong to the god."

He frowned, and gripped a hank of grass. Earth crumbled dark between his fingers as he lifted the clod. "This is a good land, and my people are hungry for a home. You said that the White Dragon would conquer."

"I do not remember—" Ambros whispered.

"Then the god gave you the words. This land will belong to us, and we to this land."

Ambros shook his head, denying it, but the stones of the barrow, that had seen so many peoples pass, told him that it was true.

Ambros did not protest when Hengest took him back to Vitalinus, nor did he repeat what the Saxon leader had told him. The Vor-Tigernus had heard the prophecy; if he did not heed Ambros when he was inspired, he was unlikely to believe what the boy said in his ordinary senses. But from that day, Ambros avoided the Saxons.

For a time, Ambros dared to hope he had been mistaken. He was growing fast now, as if the hammering he had received from the blacksmith—from Govannon himself, and Brigantia, if he had not been dreaming—had unbound his limbs, which seemed to lengthen day by day. Hengest's son Octha and a chieftain called Ebissa, who was his nephew, were sent to garrison the lands below the wall, and the Picts kept close to their own hearthfires. Ambrosius did not dare to challenge the Vor-Tigernus again.

But while Ambros gained in height, Hengest gained men. Keel after keel rowed past Tanatus to beach their boats where Caesar had landed. Others ran ashore below the white cliffs at Dubris, and their crews marched overland to Durovernum. Prince Gorangonus lived a prisoner in his own city, but the Over-King would not hear his complaints.

In the year that Ambros turned sixteen, the distant storm whose lightnings had played upon the horizon for so long broke upon the British in all its terrible power.

Cantium had been more than sufficient for Hengest's original war-band, but it could not support the horde that had followed them. Hengest no longer came to Londinium; it was Godwulf who presented his demands for more gold. But the Vor-Tigernus had already given the Saxons all the gold he had.

And so the Saxon wolves turned at last upon the poor sheep they had guarded, and all the south and east of Britannia were engulfed in blood and fire. Venta Icenorum vanished, Camulodunum was overrun; the gate of Lindum was burnt down. And if walled towns fell, how much more vulnerable were the isolated villas and farms. Where the Saxons did not strike, fear of them wielded a keen-edged sword. Everywhere folk fled, and even when the first fury of the revolt ebbed, they did not return.

But in Londinium, the Vor-Tigernus clung grimly to his imperium. The barbarians were not invincible. Even the terrible Attila had been defeated by Aetius at the Catalaunian fields. Vitalinus had sons, Vortimer and Categirnus, who were now come to manhood, and together they set out to reconquer Brittannia.

THE NIGHT OF
THE LONG KNIVES

A·D· 458

"AMBROS SON OF MADERUN, YOU ARE WELCOME TO LUGUVALIUM—"
Amlodius led the guest toward the hearth. "We have not seen
you here in the north for far too long."

Igierne resisted the temptation to whirl around to look at
him. At twenty, a married woman with a child of her own, she
was surely too mature to leap up because the Vor-Tigernus's
prophet had come. Then her father and his guest moved into
her line of sight and her eyes widened; kinsman though he
might be, she had never seen anyone like Ambros before.

His height was not so surprising—her own father was tall.
But she had never encountered so hairy a man. The hair of his
head had been trimmed, but his eyebrows bristled, and the
short beard merged with the dark hair that grew thickly on
neck and his arms below the embroidered borders of his
sleeves. No doubt his legs, covered by loose breeches of fine
wool, were furry as well. Then his swift, evaluating glance,
moving over the assembly, crossed hers. For a moment black
eyes stared into blue.

He is proud, she thought, marshalling her own self-respect to
withstand that scrutiny. *He has reason to be*. All men had heard

72

how even as a child Ambros had confounded the wise. During the Saxon wars he had become the Vor-Tigernus's most valued counselor. He wore the garments of a prince, and around his neck hung a pendant of a running stag on a chain of gold. Then his gaze passed on, and she let out her breath in a long sigh.

"Sit—" said Argantel, gesturing to a servant to bring food. "You have had a long ride."

"I have, but my lord wished to honor you by sending his message through one who is kin."

Ambros's voice was deep, with a curiously husky timbre. They said his father had not been human, and Igierne could believe it, for the red glints in his hair were the only feature he shared with his mother's kin.

"The proclamation states that we have defeated the Saxons. Horsa was killed at Rithergabail, but Hengest holds Cantium, and his son, Octha, the old Iceni lands. Is that a victory?" Amlodius asked as they sat down.

"It is all the victory we will have in this generation." Ambros threw back the folds of his mantle, a druid's cloak, checkered in many colors and held by a silver pin, and took his own seat. "He has given both his sons to defend Britannia. If the princes of the West and North would fight under his banner, the Saxons might be swept from our shores, but they will not do so, and he will not submit himself to Aurelianus. Therefore this treaty that Hengest has offered is the best outcome we are likely to achieve."

"But a partition!" exclaimed one of the other men. "It is a recognition that they will never go away."

"This Wall that you guard so carefully is a partition, but the religion and culture of Rome are found in Dun Breatann as well as in Luguvalium. Men from every part of the world have become good sons of Britannia. We will trade back and forth across that border, and in time they will learn our ways."

Amlodius laughed. "I suppose you are right. My own grandfather came from the same lands as Hengest, but I am a Roman."

"And you are one of the masters of the North. Vitalinus summons all the great lords who are sworn to him to come to Sorviodunum by the first day of May. His sons may be gone, but it will be well for the Saxons to know what strength is united against them when the treaty is made."

Amlodius frowned. Igierne had been surprised, when she arrived for this visit, to realize that his fair hair was now all turned to silver and the massive shoulders a little bowed. In contrast, her mother, despite a sprinkling of silver at the temples, seemed young. It would be a long trip for an old man, but he was nodding in agreement.

"It has been many years since I visited the South. I would like to see what the Saxons have done to the land."

"They have destroyed it," said one of the men who had come with Ambros's escort, "as the wolf who gains entry to the sheepfold in his bloodlust rends and slays far more than he can devour."

"We drove them back, but we cannot force those who fled before them to return," said another. "Good farms lie abandoned, and the towns that remain are dying, for there is no way to get the goods made in one place to market in another. And the weather has been so bad these past years it seems that even God has turned against us, and is giving the coastlands back to the sea."

The servant brought round a tray of silver cups and Argantel poured wine from a pitcher made of Roman glass. Igierne sipped appreciatively. In Dumnonia, they had wine often, brought over by the ships that traded with Gaul, but this was an old vintage, hoarded in the cellars of the Roman fort.

One of Ambros's men asked where the wine had come from, and Amlodius began to talk about the vintages he had known as a young man. With a start, she realized that Ambros was watching her. Argantel followed the direction of his gaze and smiled.

"I forget that you will not have met my daughter, Igierne."

"You are the wife of the Prince of the Dumnonii—" he

stated, as if, she thought with a spurt of irritation, he were labeling her. But she smiled sweetly in return.

Igierne had grown accustomed to being viewed as an appendage of Gorlosius when she was in Dumnonia, but returning to the North, she had begun to think of herself in the singular once more. What was he seeing, she wondered, beyond a tall woman with her father's fair hair?

"I was married three years past, and have a little daughter who is just a year old."

Morgause was auburn-haired and strong-willed like her grandmother, and Igierne loved her dearly, but it had been a relief to get away from her for a little while.

"It is well that you are both here at the same time," Argantel said softly. "You two are the only heirs in the next generation of the line of Artorius Hamicus, and it is in my mind to take this opportunity to teach you the rites of the Sword."

Ambros's eyes widened. "My mother told me its history, but I thought the priestesses—"

"On the Isle of Maidens it is guarded, but it can be touched only by those of our line. Will you come, son of Maderun, and take up the priesthood that is your heritage?"

For a moment something unfathomable stirred in his dark eyes; then they became opaque once more. He nodded, and Igierne felt her heart bound in her breast and did not know if it beat with anticipation or fear.

It was inevitable, as they rode south from Luguvalium, that Igierne should find herself often in the company of her cousin. Argantel rode in a horse-litter, but Igierne was mounted on a sturdy hill-pony, and Ambros on a bigger mount of the old cavalry breed. He was interested in her impressions of Ambrosius Aurelianus, who had guested with them several times at Bannhedos, and she, of course, was curious about Vitalinus and the Saxon woman he had married.

"She went back to her father when Hengest broke faith with the king. Among her people it is a woman's right to leave a marriage, and though they were wed in a Christian ceremony,

I think in her heart she was a heathen still. But it is true that she was very beautiful."

He frowned, and Igierne wondered if that beauty had stirred him. She had observed that he did not look at women with lust, as some men did, but rather as if they were a puzzle to be solved.

"To be pagan is not so great a sin in the North," said Igierne. "I was raised to be a priestess and my mother's heir, though it proved necessary for us to make an alliance with Dumnonia. Perhaps when I have given Gorlosius a son I will take my daughter and return here."

He looked at her curiously. "Do you not love your husband?"

The undertone of bitterness in her answer surprised her. "Love has little to do with the matings of princes. From me he expects fertility and faithfulness, and he gives me support and protection. Like most of the Dumnonian lords he has interests in Armorica. He may have a concubine there—I have never asked."

She kept her eyes on the road ahead, where the great crouching shapes of the hills guarded what lay within. The country around Luguvalium was rolling, and in Dumnonia one always felt exposed to the immensity of sky. But the Lake country was a land set apart; those whom it called to itself might find a path through the wooded dales, but the way could not be forced by an enemy.

"Among our people it was not always so," he said softly at last. "The druids teach that the king serves the land and if need be, dies for it. But it is through the queen that he touches its power. But not since the days of Brannos, I think, have we had a High King of all Britannia, and even he had no Tigernissa, no High Queen."

"My mother is Branuen, the hidden queen who performs the rites for the sake of the land, and I suppose that I will bear that mantle after her."

"But what if Branuen and Tigernissa were the same woman, a priestess-queen? Might not the king then become Brannos as well as Vor-Tigernus, a sacred king who would rule over a golden age?" His voice trembled, and turning, she saw that he too was staring at the holy hills.

"Have you seen this in a vision?" she asked softly.

"A vision?" He shook his head. "I have learned more certain ways to foretell what the future holds, and the magic, if need be, to change it."

As their journey continued, Igierne continued to consider his words. He sounded very confident, but Ambros was by his very nature a creature half of myth and magic. If he seemed arrogant perhaps he had reason. As for herself, the latest, and it seemed to her the least, in a long line of priestesses, what power could she have in a world where priestesses were becoming as legendary as the gods they had served? If men honored her it was only because she was the daughter of one great lord and the wife of another.

And yet, as they wound their way into the hills, Igierne felt herself slipping backward in time. Her mother, also, seemed to become younger as the Lake grew near. But Ambros grew strange, as if the veneer of sophistication which he had acquired in the Vor-Tigernus's court was peeling away to reveal some other being, more ancient and elemental, that lived within. He spoke less and looked around him more, and when they paused to rest the horses he would dismount and move to the edge of the forest with a grace so alien and still that she half-expected him to disappear into a tree.

On the fourth day of travel they reached the top of the pass. From here they could look down into the vale whose center was the blue lake with its tree-crowned islands.

"There lies the Holy Isle—" Igierne pointed to the largest, which lay close to the eastern shore. Here and there the gold of thatched roofs gleamed from among the trees; the long feasting hall, the roundhouses where the priestesses lived, and a little apart from the others, the House of the Sword. "We will be there by the time night falls."

"I will be glad of it," he answered harshly. "This wilderness makes me afraid."

Igierne looked at him in surprise.

"—Not of the mountains," he added then, "but of myself. When I gaze at these hills the great prophet and learned counselor of Vitalinus seems a crawling insect that one shiver of the ground could knock away. And if I am not the Vor-Tigernus's mage, what am I?"

She nodded. "I have sensed that strangeness in you. It is different for me. Here, I come into my own power."

He considered her curiously. "Is it because you are a woman, I wonder, or because—" He did not finish the thought, but turned to gaze down at the Isle of Maidens as if it could give him his answer.

As soon as he stepped through the door Ambros could scent the power. He stared around the House of the Sword, hair lifting along his spine at the growing sense that something that had been patiently waiting was now awakening. Light flickered madly across the floor as Igierne fixed torches in the sockets, and the draperies that shrouded the altar flared suddenly crimson. He found himself watching her as he had ever since he came to the North: a swift glance, swiftly turned away, lest she should see. Was it because she was a woman of his own blood that he felt drawn to her, or was there some other reason, that he was not yet ready to understand?

He heard Argantel draw a careful breath, then she pulled the cloth away from the Sword, murmuring words of praise and salutation to the spirit that lived within.

The blade stood upright in a block of stone. Perhaps half its length was free; its surface, of some polished metal that had neither tarnished nor rusted during all these years, gleamed red in the light of the fires. Ambros did not use weapons, but he had learned to judge them. The cross-guard was plain, but the hilt had been wound with gold wire. It was a sword sturdy enough to serve a warrior, with a stark elegance worthy of a king.

"I will teach you the prayers later," said the priestess. "Tonight I will do no more than introduce you. . . ." She lifted the cage which held the cockerel. "But it is for you to make the offering. Daughter, you must assist him."

Biting her lip with concentration, Igierne extracted the fowl from the cage. Ambros looked from her to her mother in confusion.

"What, have you never killed a chicken for the pot?" Argantel laughed. "Well it is time you learned!"

He blinked back vertigo. Eating at the king's table, he had never killed anything before, but he could not admit that while the women were watching him so expectantly. He took a firm grip, feeling the fowl's frantic heartbeat. Then he twisted its neck, and gasped as he *felt* the life departing. Hot blood gushed over his hands.

In the next moment his revulsion gave way to an appalling surge of hunger. Then the priestess guided his arm so that the fowl's blood dripped onto the altar stone. His own sensations paled before the approach of the god as the light of a candle dims in the sun.

Argantel was saying something, but he could not understand the words. He saw Igierne reach out, saw her face change as she grasped the hilt of the Sword. Argantel set her own hand over that of her daughter, and together they pulled the blade a handsbreadth further from the stone. Another twist, and the Sword was thrust back. Then the priestess grasped his wrist and pressed his own hand, still red with the blood of the rooster, around the hilt of the Sword.

"You must twist as you withdraw the blade . . ." her words seemed to come from a great distance, "or it will not move." Her grip tightened on his hand, but he did not need the instruction, for the blood of his great-great-grandfather was awake within him. Smoothly he turned the blade and felt it slide freely through the stone.

"Not too far—" said Argantel. "The time to draw it has not yet come."

He stared at her through eyes that he knew were rimmed white with the effort of keeping control. A voice that was

louder than the drumming in his blood began to speak in his
soul.

*"Not yet, man of the ancient blood. You are not the King who
shall wield this blade, but the time will come when you shall enable
him to claim it. Lift up your eyes, for she in whose womb he shall be
cradled stands before you. . . ."*

Ambros looked up, blinking as if he had been staring into the
light, and saw Igierne. Her face was shining, and her pale hair
flared out around her head like rays of gold, and in that moment
she was beautiful beyond mortal imagining. He stared at her,
and understood at last that for him she was the Goddess, and
that what he felt for her was love. What she heard he did not
know, but she stretched out her hand and set it upon the pom-
mel of the Sword, and together, they thrust it home.

Radiance flared around them. Dazzled, Ambros tried to look
back at Igierne, but it was the face of a boy he saw, brown-
haired and intent, with Igierne's blue eyes.

The treaty talks took place at a shrine north of Sorviodunum,
on the edge of the broad central plain. Ambros supposed it
must qualify as neutral ground, having belonged to both British and Saxons in turn during the past few years. The Saxons
had built a shelter for the meetings—no more than a frame-
work with a thatched roof to keep off the rain. Between the
posts one could look out past the last sheltering swales of grass
to the broad sweep of the plain. It was an empty land, haunted
by memories of peoples so ancient no one even remembered
their names. Perhaps that accounted for the unease that had
troubled him since the meetings began.

They had feasted on beef and pork, a raider's menu. The
rich scent of roast meat still hung in the air. But now, at last,
the eating was over. When the drinking horns had gone round
a few times for men to toast the new treaty, it would be done.

They sat at long trestle tables covered with an assortment of
cloths. Hengest, to emphasize the peaceful nature of this festival, had forbidden the usual barbarian custom in which men
came armed to a feast and hung sword and shield behind them

on the wallposts. But the Saxons still looked like savages. Ambros sighed, remembering the last time he had come to Sorviodunum with the Vor-Tigernus, when he was still a child. They had dined in one of the great houses of the town, and eaten off the elegant table service that had once belonged to the Roman magistrates. Its pieces were probably scattered through half the Saxon army by now.

Not, strictly speaking, that it was all Saxon any more. The chieftain sitting next to Amlodius was Aelle, whose Saxons had settled into the coastal lands to the east of Noviomagus. But Hengest himself had peopled Cantium with Jutes and Frisians. There were Franks as well, and others whose names he did not know. The ravens who feasted on the carcass of Britannia were drawn from half a dozen northern tribes, paired one by one with the British councilors.

Ambros pushed the meat on his platter distastefully aside. *Ah Vortimer*, he thought, *we should have honored your dying wish and buried you on the eastern shore. Then, perhaps, your spirit would have saved us from this day . . .*

His own dinner partner was Godwulf, who had once taught him the Eruli lore. The Saxon thyle had always been hard to read, but tonight he seemed as impenetrable as Hadrian's wall. In the days when he had cast runes for Vitalinus, Ambros had thought him old. But by now Godwulf must be in his eighties, a truly remarkable age.

"You are in health, I see. Your gods have been good to you," Ambros said politely.

Godwulf smiled. He was missing some of his teeth, and could only eat his food chopped fine. It gave him a more sinister appearance than Ambros remembered.

"It is so," the old man answered. "Woden gives victory in the battles of the mind as well as those of the body, and he likes this land. You should make him an offering."

Ambros lifted one eyebrow. Powerful the god might be, but all his help had no more than won his people a toehold in Britannia.

"You may offer to your demon, and I will honor mine," he

said wryly, for the Christian priests would characterize the heathen god and the spirit that spoke to him in his soul alike as devils.

Or that used to speak to him. These days, he commanded spirits rather than praying to them. He tried to remember how long it had been since his inner voice had counseled him.

"If different peoples are to live in peace, their gods must make peace as well," unfazed, Godwulf was answering. "So it was when Woden and the Ase-gods fought with the Wanes. Neither side could conquer, and so they became allies."

"Do you mean to put an eyepatch on Lugos and call him Woden-Lugos, as the Romans used to honor Mars-Belutacadros and many another, proclaiming that all the deities of the peoples they conquered were only faces of their own? They are not the same!"

"Your Lugos is not Woden, not as we encounter him, though they both carry a sacred spear," agreed the thyle, "but there is a place where they meet. Those who can come there will understand how disparate peoples can become one."

"Is Hengest such a man?" asked Ambros, looking at the high table. The Saxon leader sat next to Vitalinus, like an old stallion, scarred and gaunt, looming over a grizzled fox. He sat at his ease, but his eyes were watchful, like a man awaiting the beginning of battle, not one who sighs relief at its ending. Once more, Ambros felt that little prickle of unease.

"Hengest loves this land . . ." Godwulf said ambiguously.

"Will he honor the treaty, now that we have given him what he asked?"

"He will keep the oaths he swears on the sacred ring." The thyle touched the silver arm-ring, graven over with runes, that he wore.

Ambros nodded. It was the oath-taking, not the writing of words on parchment, that would bind the Saxon.

A serving lad bore the mead pitcher past the benches and refilled his beaker. Ordinarily Ambros did not drink deeply, but he had felt the strain of this long war more deeply than he realized, and drinking brought release. He looked at the other

British lords and saw that for them it was the same. Faces grew flushed and voices louder; laughter filled the air. The Saxons, eyes bright with excitement, were laughing too, but they were accustomed to deep drinking. Indeed, they were being remarkably temperate this evening, as if they feared to shame themselves.

The platters of roasted meat were taken away, and the ill-assorted collection of plates. Did the fact that nothing matched matter to the Saxons? Ambros thought of a Saxon warrior he had seen emerging from a burning village, wearing a Roman helmet and a woman's gown. Perhaps they liked the variety. Perhaps they were naturally perverse. . . . He realized that the mead was affecting him and set down his beaker.

"It is good mead," said Godwulf.

"It is indeed, but do not your own shopes warn against allowing the heron of heedlessness to steal a man's wits away?"

"You are, as always, wise," said Godwulf with a peculiar smile. He swung himself around and eased off the bench. At the high table, Vitalinus had risen to face the man who had been first his greatest servant and then his greatest foe. A priest stood behind him, holiding a reliquary. Gradually a hush spread through the crowd.

The Vor-Tigernus set one hand upon the casket. He looked sour, but determined, as befitted a man who was about to swear part of his native land away.

"We have labored as hard to frame this treaty as ever we fought on the battlefield," he said. "And all the harder, because our goal was not victory, but a settlement that would be fair to both sides. The details are written, but to this I will now take oath: that the lands which were formerly those of the Iceni and the Cantiaci shall belong to the Saxons and Angles who now dwell therein, and such other smaller enclaves as are specified in the treaty. I pledge that my people will honor their tenure and recognize their borders. In the name of the Father, Son, and Holy Spirit." He crossed himself, a gesture which was echoed by most of the British lords.

Godwulf drew the oath-ring from his arm and held it out to Hengest.

"On the ring of Thunor I swear, and in the name of Woden—this land that we have taken, we shall hold—and as much more as the gods shall give into our hand!"

He released the arm-ring, and turning, held out his arms to Vitalinus as if to embrace him. *"Nimet oure seaxes!"* he cried.

Vitalinus recoiled, but with another step the Saxon swept him into a bear hug that carried him away from the high table and toward the end of the hall.

Staring in amazement, Ambros caught the first flicker of movement only from the corner of his eye. Then someone screamed. Steel flashed in the light of the torches—a dagger, when by agreement all men had come unweaponed to this feast. Coelius of Eburacum and three others lay sprawled in their blood already. But the Saxons were not having it all their own way. Those who had not been felled in the first moments still struggled with the men who by chance or design had been placed to partner them, who had shared the same meat and mead, making missiles of their drinking horns or laying about them with benches. Eldaul of Glevum had pulled up a tent stake and was using it like a club.

Following his example, Ambros wrenched a post from the ground and started toward the nearest Saxons, but Godwulf was before him. As Ambros started to swing, the thyle pulled a short wand from his belt and swiftly drew several symbols in the air.

"Eees—" The thyle drew out the syllables of the bind-rune in a pulsing drone. *"Nyd—"*

Ambros felt the air congeal around him; he could still move, but slowly, far too slowly, like a man struggling through a storm.

Why not kill me? Ambros's mind raced. Did the old man hesitate to murder one who had been his pupil; or did he lack the power? With that thought, Ambros summoned his own energies, drawing on earth and air as Maugantius had taught him, and where they met in his solar plexus, kindling a fire that shocked through every limb.

In another moment he could move again, but in those few minutes the British princes had passed beyond his aid. Men lay sprawled all about him, silent in death or groaning while their murderers stood panting above them, still clutching the dripping daggers they had brought hidden beneath their leggings when they came to the hall.

Ambros forced stiff limbs to carry him across the ground to Amlodius. His cousin's husband still breathed, but life was ebbing out of him from many wounds, and blood frothed at his lips with every gasp. An animal moan of dismay passed Ambros's own lips as he bent over him, pressing a corner of the older man's mantle over the worst of the wounds.

"No use . . ." The whisper was almost too faint to hear. "Tell Argantel . . . choose Caidiau to rule in . . . Lugu—"

If Amlodius completed the word, it was too softly for Ambros to hear. His gaze became fixed, and then the soul-light faded like a dying flame and was gone.

Slowly, Ambros lifted the old man's body in his arms and got to his feet. The air vibrated with the passage of spirits reft untimely from the flesh that had housed them; they made a roaring in his ears that drowned out all other sound. Where his gaze fell men flinched, but he had no interest in lesser murderers, even Aelle. It was Hengest whom his eyes sought, standing like a deity of carnage in the midst of the slain. Vitalinus, his arms pinioned by a grinning warrior, stood beside him, weeping and shouting words that Ambros could not hear.

He drew breath, and Godwulf, eyes widening, lifted his staff and began to draw runes of protection. But the spells of the thyle could no longer hold him. Ambros opened his mouth and released the words that all those wailing spirits no longer had breath to say—

"In the name of Britannia's gods I curse you, and by the power of all the spirits of this land!" Power shuddered through him and he recognized the oncoming Presence he had sensed when Argantel showed him the Sword. This was not the gentle wisdom of his daimon, but a force that expanded his aura beyond even his own great height.

"Hear Me, men of the forests and fens and hear Me, you who lead them." The voice of the god boomed through the hall. "As you have been false to your trust, so shall you be betrayed by those you trusted. As you have usurped the lordship of this land, the leadership of those peoples you have brought here shall be given to another! You have slain the flower of Britannia, but from their bones a host shall rise up to confront you. I will raise up a Defender, and he will strike you with a Sword of Fire!"

Ambros could not hear the sound of his own words, but Hengest heard them. Yet if some of the triumph left his face, it was replaced by a stubborn pride that would neither defend nor deny what he had done.

The warrior who was holding Vitalinus let him go, and the old man sank weeping to the floor, a dead man who still moved and breathed. Ambros wondered if the god would curse him too, but there was no point to it; the man who had been the Vor-Tigernus had destroyed himself, the White Dragon savaging the Red as Ambros himself had foretold so long ago. His very name would be a curse so long as Britannia endured.

He swayed as the power of the god began to leave him, but enough strength remained for him to bear the body of his kinsman through the door, and no man sought to bar his way.

"Ambros, what has happened? They told me you had come to the Lake, but not your errand. Is my lord—"

Argantel's brisk greeting faltered. Something in Ambros's face must be conveying the message for which he could not yet find words.

"You have had no news?" he asked hoarsely.

"Neither enemies nor news of them can find their way to this holy place without my will." Her words were proud, but he could see the beginnings of a stricken look in her eyes. His mother had said once that Argantel's marriage had been a political arrangement. But the priestess had come to care for her Roman commander.

"I have brought your husband home."

Once more his throat closed. His memories of that journey were confused. In Sorviodunum he had found a man who would build him a coffin, and a wagon to bear it, and up the Great North Road he had driven, pausing only to rest and feed the horse, neither knowing nor caring what tales might follow him. It occurred to him now that the goal of bringing Amlodius back to his people was the only thing that had kept him sane.

But Argantel was a priestess, accustomed to reading men's souls.

"He is dead?" Her voice cracked on the words. She must be guessing already that no simple illness or stopping of the heart would have made Ambros bring him here himself, and in such a state as this.

"They are all dead—" Ambros whispered. "The Saxons killed—" he gasped, and then, like water breaking through a dam, all the dreadful tale poured out of him at last.

He was weeping by the time he finished. Argantel remained calm, but her stillness seemed the quiet of an autumn forest silvered by a sudden frost. She gave orders for the coffin to be brought into the sanctuary and the horse to be cared for. Hot spiced ale was offered and Ambros drank it gratefully, but when she showed him a bed he shook his head.

"I cannot rest, not yet. I have pushed too hard and long. Perhaps if I walk along the shore I will find peace. . . ."

Argantel nodded. "If there is peace anywhere it is here. Thank you for bringing Amlodius back to me."

Ambros stared at her. Didn't she understand? If not for him, her husband would never have gone into danger. She lifted her hand in blessing and left him, and he saw that in those few moments she had become old.

He took up his cloak and went out, turning down the path that led to the shore. The Isle of Maidens was no more than a few boat-lengths from the mainland. The flat-bottomed barge that had brought over his wagon lay drawn up on shore. He turned away from it and began to pick his way among the rocks that edged the water.

Hills rose sheer to the south and west and north, dark shapes humped like sleeping beasts against the starlit sky. By habit his gaze found the pole star and he marked the constellations around it. He could name the fixed stars and those that wandered, foretell their conjunctions and oppositions, but he had failed to read Hengest's heart. He was a fraud and a failure, all his vaunted wisdom worth nothing. He had been a better prophet when he was seven years old!

Ambros looked back at the clustered buildings. By morning they would all have heard the news and know how he had failed. Indeed, by now all Britannia must know how the Vor-Tigernus's prophet had walked into the trap and stood gaping while the princes of Britannia were slain.

How could he face them? How could he face *anyone* now?

Before him the dark waters lapped quietly at the shore. Let them swallow him, he thought numbly, and drown his shame. . . .

Ambros let his cloak fall to the ground and moved forward. The water was very cold, but it did not stop him. Steadily he continued as the water rose to his knees, his waist, his chest. In another moment it would close over his head and he would be at peace.

But instead it receded to his waist again. The lake bottom was rising. For a moment he stood undecided, but if he returned to the island now he would appear not only a failure but a fool. Perhaps the shadows of the forest would be deep enough to engulf him. Shivering, he pushed forward, and when he reached the shore he kept going, blundering blindly on.

Several times during that night he fell, and lay for a time in mindless exhaustion. But always a moment would come when self-awareness returned, and the voices in his head would begin to accuse him once more. Then he would stagger to his feet and push onward. By the time dawn banished the darkness he had covered many miles. He burrowed into a tangle of vines then and sleep delivered him from his accusers at last.

When he awoke, he was aware only of hunger. A heedless squirrel came within his reach, and he, who in all his life had killed only the cockerel he had offered to the god in the Sword, pounced on it and tore it to pieces, ripping off the pelt, crunching up flesh and bone. Wild onion grew nearby and he ate that too, and lapped water, wolf-fashion, from the stream. Then he began to move once more, south and westward, ever deeper into the hills.

As day followed day, the voices grew fainter, and after a time he ceased to think in words at all. His body hardened and he no longer noticed the cold. The strange flapping things that covered his limbs became encumbrances, and he tore them off and threw them away. He became more clever at foraging for food, though he never found quite enough to satisfy his large frame.

He saw deer, and once a thrown rock even brought one down. He smelled bear and avoided them, and became acquainted with beaver and badger and the wild pig and wolf that roamed these hills. One day he came upon a new creature, furred like a beast but standing upright in the rapids to snatch fish from the stream. As he approached it took fright and ran off, still on two legs, and he came down to the waterside to drink.

The backwater was still. As he bent, something moved in its depths and he jumped back. Then, more cautious, he leaned over the water, and saw a creature covered with bristling hair. It strongly resembled the one that had run away.

Wild Man. . . . A distant memory stirred of men dressed in garments tufted with colored yarn who ran shouting through the streets at festivals. And in that moment of clarity he understood of what blood he himself was come.

Were there more than the one he had seen, and would they accept him among them? He sat back on his haunches, the realization that he was himself a beast making it possible, for the first time in weeks, to think like a man.

Sunlight glanced blindingly from the water; he blinked and stilled, for someone was standing there. Not a Wild Man; it was a human woman's form, veiled in shining hair. She turned and he saw a face he remembered from dreams. When she spoke it was the voice he had so often heard in his soul. Among human women, only Igierne had ever stirred his heart. But this being touched a place that lay deeper still.

"It is so—you stand between the worlds of beast and man, and you can choose what you will be. You are a mule, and will have no offspring of your body, but if you return to humankind you will have a child of the spirit, and he will be the greatest of Britannia's kings."

His throat worked as he struggled to form human words.

"If I go, will you be with me?"

"If you will open your heart," she answered, "for I am the Bride of your Soul, and in truth I have never been far away."

The angle of the sun changed and the vision vanished. But he could still feel her presence. He waded into the river and began to scrub the dirt away. Then, when he was as clean as he could manage, he started out again, not back to the Isle of Maidens, but south, to Ambrosius Aurelianus and his brother Uthir, who were now the undisputed leaders of Britannia.

THE DRAGON STAR

A·D· 459

"YOU HAVE SINNED AGAINST THE LORD OF HOSTS, AND THE DEVIL has sent his legions to chastise you!" The tattered sleeves of a robe that had once been white fluttered as the priest shook his fists against the sunset sky. "For your greed you are punished; for your faithlessness you are cast down. You have followed the heretic Pelagius, and thought that your own deeds could save you, and this is the result—rivers running with blood and a land in flames!" Spittle flew from parched lips as the priest brought down his arms.

"It is true!" wailed the people. "We have sinned! We must flee this accursed land!"

The tall figure at the edge of the crowd moved forward, leaning on his rowan staff. These days he called himself Merlin, the name that "son of Maderun," misheard, had become. He did not trouble to correct it. Ambros had been a human name, and that man had died in the forest. It seemed fitting that he, who was not really a man, should bear what was not a real name.

Merlin had come into the wayfarers' encampment hoping for food and fire—this close to midsummer a day's journey was long. Instead, he had found this haranguing cleric, whose whine made him want to turn back to the quiet of the hills.

"You sought to cast out the devil Hengest, and as happened to the man from whom they cast out the devil, seven demons worse than the first one have invaded our land!" the priest was continuing.

And that was true enough, for the German tribesmen who had hung back when Vortimer was battling Hengest to a standstill had come howling like wolves to tear at the poor bleeding carcass of Britannia once the way was opened by treachery. Aelle and his sons held the lands east of Sorviodunum, and the Jutes and Frisians had taken back all their old lands in Cantium and more. The walled cities of Londinium, Verulamium, Regnum and many others still held, but throughout the eastern half of the country the enemy ranged freely.

"Should we have welcomed the Saxon?" asked someone, and a few people grimaced with what might have been laughter if they had not forgotten how.

In truth, they were a sorry lot; even those who had fled with some of their wealth were worn and dirty. The skin on the priest's face hung in folds, as if he had once been a much heavier man. Those whom Merlin passed edged aside, crossing themselves. He had become accustomed to that, for if they were tattered caricatures of their former prosperity, he had abandoned all its trappings, and now went barefoot, in a garment of deerskin, mantled with a wolf's hide that he pinned with the curving tusk of a wild boar. But he knew how to veil his presence so that even those men who had been startled by his appearance in another moment forgot what they had seen.

"Leave the land to the sea wolves, and may they have joy of it," answered another. "We'll make a new home in Armorica."

Many of his countrymen had done so already, following the men whom the Emperor Maximian had led away two generations before. War and plague had left Armorica nearly empty, and Riothamus, who ruled there now, welcomed the men of Britannia.

"Will you leave the land to the wolves, or to those who still have the balls to fight for it?" A new voice cut through the babble of agreement.

Merlin turned. Several horsemen had pulled up at the edge of the firelight. The speaker urged his mount a few steps forward, and they saw a big man with mouse-brown hair cut short in the Roman manner, a weatherstained crimson cavalry cloak wrapped over his mail.

"Where are your sentries?" snapped the officer, or rather, the prince, for as he moved Merlin glimpsed at his throat a torc of gold. Three of the men at the outskirts of the crowd hung their heads. "We'd have caught you with your breeches down had we been Saxons!"

"My lord, you have no right to talk to us this way!" the priest exclaimed.

"Do I not?" The prince urged his horse through the crowd until he was almost on top of the cleric. "My brother and I were already safe *in* Armorica! You called us back to Britannia, promised to stand behind us if we would lead you. And now we are here, and when *we* start to plough a furrow, we don't leave the job half done!" He made an obscene gesture that left no doubt of his meaning.

Some of the men looked shamefaced, but others faced the prince with a mutinous glare.

"God Himself has cursed this land. Who are we to fight against the will of God?"

The prince glared in frustration. Clearly, if calling men cowards did not move them, he was at a loss for persuasions. Merlin smiled. He had met neither Aurelianus nor Uthir, but this must be the younger brother, for the emperor was said to be a man of some subtlety. One virtue they both had was energy. They had hunted Vitalinus down already and burned him in his tower.

Then Uthir turned, and Merlin's breath caught as memory overlaid that face with another, seen once in vision, with Igierne's blue eyes.

This was the man who would beget the Defender.

Merlin surveyed him with new interest, searching for lines

of character in the pleasant face, for a strength of will to match the powerful body. He saw endurance and determination there; it was the face of a good commander. But was there greatness? He could not tell, but then he had not seen the treachery in Hengest's soul. His own judgment had proved lacking, and he could only trust the gods.

"Blame God for the storm that drowns your crops, but not for the fear that makes you flee." He allowed the power of his personality to blaze forth so that to the people, noticing him for the first time, it was as if he had appeared among them by magic. Even Uthir's horse tossed its head in surprise and had to be reined down.

"Rome protected you as a parent protects a growing child. But now Mother Rome is gone. Will you cling to her skirts when she can no longer even guard herself, or will you defend yourselves like men? Fleeing to Armorica will not save you— the barbarians are everywhere. If you do not stand together to fight them here you will have to do it later, in a foreign land."

"Who are you to condemn us?" someone cried.

"I am no man's son and no man's father . . ." Merlin's voice rang out through the darkness. "I have been a wolf on the hills and a stag in the meadow. . . . I soar with the eagle and root with the wild boar beneath the ground. I am the Wild Man of the woods and the prophet of Britannia, and my spirits tell me what is to come. . . ."

"Prophesy the future, then!"

"Why should I prophesy what logic can reveal?" Merlin asked contemptuously. "The mysteries of heaven cannot be revealed except where there is the most pressing need for them. If I were to utter them as an entertainment or where there is no necessity, the spirit which controls me would forsake me in the moment of need."

But as he drew breath to continue, he felt the dizzying shift in awareness that told him his daimon was awakening. His face must have changed then, for the man stood openmouthed as Merlin put the knowledge that was coming to him into words.

"You would do better to search your own heart than to question me. Confess yourself to this whining priest while you can, for this much is given to me to say—neither here nor in Armorica can you evade your doom. This very night you shall stand before your God!"

"You dare to curse—" the priest began, but Merlin's gesture silenced him.

"I neither curse nor bless. I only say what I see." He turned back toward the prince.

Sputtering, the heckler started toward him, fist raised. No man could say precisely what happened after, whether the fellow tripped and hit his head, or if he was felled by some invisible foe. But it was certain that when they lifted him up again he was dead and staring.

"Sorcery!" came the whisper, but it was not a loud one, and no one raised a hand to stop Merlin as he continued to Uthir's side.

The prince had gone pale beneath his tan, but he was not one to waste an opportunity.

"Death can strike you anywhere—" he said in a strong voice. "March with me, and if you die, at least it will be *for* something, not running away. Any man who can stiffen his rod to beget a child should be able to stiffen his spine enough to defend it. March with me, and your sons and your daughters will grow up free in their own land!"

Uthir's gaze met Merlin's as the whispers became a babble of discussion. "I know you now. You were Vitalinus's prophet. You will come with me to the emperor."

"I offer you my service."

"I hope you serve us better than you did him," said Uthir, but mingled with the trouble in his eyes was a hope that had not been there before.

North of Sorviodunum, the land rose to a broad plain. Even in more peaceful times it had been sparsely populated, and now it was nearly empty. But ghosts whispered on the wind. There were more ghosts now, thought Merlin, looking at the covered carts that the emperor's men were driving up the track from the shrine. He could sense the spirits of the British princes hovering over those mingled fragments of ash and bone.

Did Aurelianus understand what fulfilling this task, the first the emperor had asked, would cost Merlin? To other men, Sorviodunum, battle-scarred but bravely flaunting a few remnants of past glory, might be no different than any other place recaptured from the enemy; but for him, its population of dead was more numerous than the living, and more vivid, and the ghost of the man he himself had been was the most terrible of all.

To come before the emperor in Sorviodunum was hard. To ride with him to the shrine on the edge of the plain where Hengest had slain the princes was harder still. About the round huts where the monks lived, a military camp was growing. They called it Ambrosiacum now, or Ambrosius's hill.

The Saxons had burned the thatched shelter above the bodies, and though the monks had chanted prayers over them, they had no cemetery. And so Aurelianus had decreed that the princes must have a monument. To create it was Merlin's penance, and the first test of his wisdom.

One of the riders in the lead lifted his lance, pointing. Uthir kicked his horse alongside Merlin's.

"Where is the place?"

The shallow valley that the Abona had carved through the plain was falling away behind them. Ahead of them, grass and heath stretched away toward a line of hills, broken with occasional clumps of trees. Merlin pointed.

"Do you see that lump, perhaps a mile from here? That is the first mound, though indeed, such ancient burials are scattered throughout the plain. But these form a line that points back to Sorviodunum, and extends northward up the backbone of Britannia. East to West, another line passes through the Giant's Dance, and links it to the Isle of Glass, which is also a place of ancient power."

He had first come here with Maugantius during one of the Vor-Tigernus's visits to Sorviodunum, when he was a child.

The wide plain had frightened and exalted him then; it continued to do so now.

"What did you tell my brother to get him to come here?" asked Uthir.

Both of them glanced back at the horse-litter in which Ambrosius Aurelianus was following. The emperor was considerably older than his brother, and at times his joints pained him too greatly for riding to be easy. But there was nothing wrong with his mind.

"I told him that this is the most important focus of power in this part of the island," said Merlin. "The spirits whose bones are laid to rest in this place will join with those who were buried here in ancient days."

"Now, this is the border of Britannia," said Uthir with a sigh. "We don't even call ourselves Britons any longer, but *Combrogi*, the countrymen." He was an interesting contrast to his brother. Both had been educated by Greek tutors, but Uthir, perhaps to distinguish himself from the emperor, had adopted the rough language of the soldiers he commanded.

They rode on a little further, and Uthir stiffened in the saddle, pointing. "What is that?"

Out of the grass dark shapes were rising. A few more steps and they became a circle of standing stones, linked uprights surrounding grouped trilithons. The Romans had built works of greater height and complexity, but never with such massive blocks of stone. Stark against the empty plain, the henge waited with a brooding power.

"That is the Giant's Dance."

As the days shortened toward Samhain the men labored, and when they were finished, the line of barrows was longer by one. Beneath it lay the remains of the leaders of Britannia. On the eve of the Festival, Merlin commanded the workmen to build a circle of fires around the barrow and then to withdraw to the river, leaving the fires to burn through the night.

"I will go to the stone circle and make the magic that will bind these spirits to the land."

"Do you have to go alone?" asked Uthir, and Merlin raised one eyebrow, for on such a night any other man would have covered himself with protective charms and huddled by the fire. "If not, I'll go with you."

"As will I," the emperor echoed him.

Merlin bowed. He had not yet had much chance to know Aurelianus, but though the emperor's body was not strong, it was from him that Uthir had gotten his strength of will. He could see already that if Vitalinus had possessed such a purity of purpose, and such ability to make men follow him, the Saxons would never have gained a foothold in Britannia.

"For lesser men it would not be safe. But it is fitting that the kings who rule now should stand where the chieftains of ancient times held sway."

"Was this a druid temple?" Uthir had asked as they passed beneath the portal of stone.

"A temple of sorts, but not made by the druids, though they learned some of its secrets. It was built before ever our people came to this land."

"Was it the Trojans, as some have said, or wise men from Egypt who taught the people how to raise these stones?" asked Aurelianus. Well-wrapped in cloaks against the chill, he sat throned on one of the fallen stones.

"The traditions I was taught say it was neither," answered Merlin. "The mages who built the stone circles came from the west, from a land of magic far across the sea. To Eriu they came and then to Britannia. It is from these isles that the knowledge was carried southward, all the way to the lands around the Middle Sea."

It was almost midnight. They looked across the grass to the fires that circled the mound, and then up at the starry radiance of the sky.

"The stars are like the watchfires of a great host encamped in the heavens," said Uthir. "Will those spirit warriors come to help us in our need?"

"They will come if I call them. You must keep silence now, no matter what you see or hear." Merlin drew from his pouch a handful of herbs and sprinkled them in a protective circle around the princes. Then, chanting softly, he paced sunwise around the henge. As he reached each stone, he saluted it, and within the lichened rock he seemed to see the beginnings of an answering glow. The henge was awakening.

He stripped off his own clothing, laid his wolfskin on the ground halfway between the two pairs of trilithons, and sat cross-legged on the hide. He gazed upward, watching as the great round of the sky wheeled towards the sacred hour, and in the moment when the stars stood still in mid-heaven, the spirit awakened within him and he began to sing.

> Bright-shining stars, brilliant above,
> As fires of foemen burn below,
> Silent, you shall tell your story;
> Stones shall sing histories. . . .

He remembered that night he had spent in the barrow with the smith when he was a child. Then the visions had come uncontrolled and unexpected. Now he was a man in the fullness of his power, and he called them. He sang, and slowly the shining shapes began to come forth from the mounds.

He heard the rhythmic chanting of many voices as men strained to pull the massive blocks over the ground. Stone by stone, the circle was completed. He saw the blood of bulls poured out to bless them; he saw kings with gold upon their shoulders, and queens with gold twined in their curling hair. Season by season he saw the ceremonies; the inaugurations and burials and the foot races and chariot races around the mounds.

All these things he saw; these things he sang, and as the stars began to pale with the approach of dawn, he summoned the spirits.

"You who have loved this land, defend it from those who would destroy. You whose bones have become this earth, defend it from the death-bringers. You who have dwelt here in a time before time, welcome the spirits who are newly come to your realm!"

The glow from the stones grew brighter, raying out across the plain. Where it fell, transparent figures rose from the earth, more and more of them with every moment. As the wind lifts the leaves, his song moved them toward the new mound. In the east the sky grew bright with the approach of dawn. The fires were veiled by an opalescent cloud, swirling ever more swiftly until the earth of the barrow opened and the spirits of the newly dead burst free.

In that instant the burning edge of the sun rimmed the horizon. Merlin heard a gasp of awe from behind him; then he blinked at the explosion of radiance above the mound. The sun lifted free of earth's shadow and light flamed in a burning path from the mound across the grass to flare from the stones of the henge.

The living and the dead and the earth itself joined in a great shout of praise. Merlin felt his spirit reft away in a timeless moment of unity. Then he fell back into his body, and sat up, blinking at the morning light of Samhain Day.

"Their sacrifice has been accepted," said a voice behind him. "They are one with the land."

It was Aurelianus, his face still radiant with awe. He looked younger than Merlin had yet seen him, but fragile, as if the spirit within him burned too fiercely for his flesh to bear. He knew then that the emperor would not live long. Uthir stood beside him, steadying his elbow.

This was the king that he would serve, thought Merlin, until the time for the Defender should come.

"They would ask no greater honor," said Uthir, "nor would I."

From that day, Merlin rode with Uthir's band. While Aurelianus traveled back to Venta to direct the defense of Britannia along the new frontier, his brother marched toward Demetia. While the combrogi had been focused on defending their eastern territories, the Picts and Scotii—the ancient enemy—took advantage of the situation to renew their raiding. Their numbers were reinforced by a band of Saxons led by Pascentius, who had been beaten off by Amlodius the year before, and had taken refuge in Eriu.

For a time, the heavens themselves seemed to be fighting on the side of their foes, for clouds rolled in from the west, washing out tracks and slowing the combrogi army. Uthir rallied them with cheerful obscenities and said that the storms had been sent by God to pin the enemy down until they could catch up with him. He was, observed Merlin, a good commander, willing to listen to advice when there was time and decisive when there was not. He asked his men to endure no hardship that he himself did not share.

As the campaign continued, Merlin grew to know the other commanders as well, Caius Turpilius, whose family had a prosperous estate near Venta Silurum and still held to the old Roman ways; Eldaul of Glevum the younger, a distant cousin of Vitalinus who always sought the most dangerous fighting in an attempt to avenge his father, and Gorlosius of the Cornovii, eldest son and heir of Gerontius, who ruled Dumnonia. Igierne's husband.

Merlin studied him more closely than the others, and found little to like, though there was much to admire. He too fought fiercely, though it seemed sometimes that his ruthlessness came from outrage that anyone would dare to oppose him. If ever Merlin had thought of offering Igierne more than a kinsman's love, recognition of his own origins would have prevented it, but it galled him to think of her bound to this arrogant princeling, when she was herself the equal of a queen.

They had marched all the way through Demetia and were pushing up the coast toward Guenet before the clouds began to break up and they saw the naked heavens once more.

When they made camp that evening, the only remains of the storm were a few tattered banners of flame across the sky. Merlin—whose usual reaction to rain was to bundle his leather clothing into a chest and go clad only in the twist of linen about his loins—was salving a sore where the wet saddle blanket had galled his pony, when he heard a shout. It was not the standard alarm for an approaching enemy. He turned and saw men pointing at the heavens.

Half these men had been shepherds before the wars. Even the farmers among them were accustomed to tell the seasons by searching the skies. Merlin had been making regular observations since Maugantius began to teach him when he was ten years old. It took no more than a moment for him to see what they were looking at—a brilliant point of light in the southeast where there had been no star before. For an hour it was visible in the heavens, then it sank behind the trees.

The next night it was brighter still, and they could see a blur of light behind it. It was a comet, Merlin told them, such as often foretold events of great import. But it was still rising. They must wait until it reached full magnitude before he could attempt to discover what it might mean.

The three nights that followed were overcast. The combrogi pushed northward, eager to come to grips with the foe. Smoke still rose from the burned timbers of the looted farmsteads they were passing now. The enemy army could not be far away.

The next day a wind came up that tossed the treetops and scoured the clouds from the sky. They made camp early that evening, choosing a rise with a clear view to the south. Merlin put on a good tunic of white wool that Aurelianus had given him; it made no difference to the magic, but to look like a druid would inspire confidence. By now, he himself was as anxious to know the comet's meaning as any of the men. But mingled with his anticipation was fear.

As daylight faded the tension grew. Merlin felt their apprehension as a pressure against his awareness and braced his mind against it. His discomfort lessened, but so did his ability to perceive the subtle currents of the universe. Frowning, he chose a good vantage point on the hill and drew the circle of herbs around him. Not even Uthir would dare to cross it, and as he closed it he felt the strain ease.

He took his place upon the wolfhide, breathing deeply and regularly and rooting his soul in the earth below. He sensed the delicate branchings of power that nourished the land; but they were only tributaries, not a mighty river such as he had tapped at the Giant's Dance. Yet even these tiny channels were troubled. Some change was coming, and soon.

The blue of the sky deepened to a luminous cobalt. The first stars gleamed suddenly, but where had the comet gone? A murmur from the men brought his attention upward and he realized that it was traveling more quickly than he had expected, for it was already high. Merlin lay back, gazing upward and, anchored by his link to the earth, allowed his spirit to soar.

The head of the comet blazed more brightly than Venus when she is the morning star, and its tail seemed to stretch halfway across the sky. Transfixed by its beauty, it took Merlin a little while to realize that someone was calling him.

"Prophet, tell me—" Uthir's voice was thin with strain, "what is this wild star?"

Already half-tranced, Merlin responded to the note of command as a horse obeys the rein. Awareness of the outer world faded; he stared up at the comet until it filled his vision. Its head had seemed a ball of light, but now it was pulsing wildly, and suddenly it was the head of a dragon. Distantly he heard his own voice reporting what he saw.

There was a mutter of awe from the men around him. Then the prince spoke again.

"Such marvels don't come by chance. What does this one mean?"

At the question, knowledge cascaded into conscious awareness with an intensity that brought Merlin upright, tears welling in his eyes.

"Woe and sorrow," he whispered, "woe and weeping for you, my lord, and for all Britannia. Your brother is dead. The noble prince is gone, and the people left without their leader." Blindly he turned toward Uthir and stretched out his hand. "Arise, son of Ambrosius, and hasten to strike your foe. Go now, while the head of the Dragon rules the sky and promises you victory. Destroy your enemy and take Britannia into your keeping."

He gazed upward once more and saw the mouth of the Dragon opening, and from its jaws blazed a tongue of fire. "You will have victory!" he shouted suddenly, "and a son greater even than his father who will save his people and win fame unending!"

Now others were clamoring, asking how Aurelianus had died, where the enemy was, what they should do. Merlin shook his head, striving to hear the voice that spoke within.

"You shall find your foes camped on the shore where the Isle of the Dead guards the bay—" he whispered. "March now, and take them as they are sleeping. You must move swiftly, for they mean to sail on the morning tide!"

They marched through the night, and the Dragon blazed above them, showing the way. And just as it was growing ghostly with the approach of dawn, the combrogi army wound down from the hills above Madoc's Bay and saw the enemy encampment sprawled across the sands below. They had sent out scouts, and every man knew what to expect and what he must do.

Except for Merlin. Uthir had made it quite clear that he must not risk himself. In any case he had never learned how men fought with weapons of iron, and he had been taught that to use his other gifts to take life would destroy both those gifts, and him. He waited on the brow of the hill, in the shelter of a thornbush. To an enemy passing by he would have been invisible, but his prophecy had brought these men to battle; he owed it to them to watch them fight.

The raiders had thought themselves safe. But they were not stupid. As Uthir's force came sweeping down the hill, guards gave the alarm, and men burst from their rude shelters or struggled free from the cloaks in which they had wrapped themselves to sleep, weapons in hand. Uthir had divided his men into three wings; one to strike from each side and the third to circle round to the shore. In such confusion the horses gave little advantage. After the first wild ride through the encampment, stabbing with lance and spear, most of the riders slid off their mounts and began to lay about them with their swords.

Surprise had evened the odds, but the enemy fought well, and all the more so when the men Uthir had delegated to the task waded out with torches and fired the vessels waiting to carry them away. Most of the plunder had already been loaded into them. Deprived of both escape and reward, the enemy had little to lose, but Uthir was determined that this lot of raiders would not return another day.

The prince had kept his mount. From the hill, Merlin marked him, reining the bay mare in tight circles, stabbing with his lance as if each man he faced was responsible for Aurelianus's loss. It was one way to deal with grief, or at least to put off facing it. The true pain would come later on.

Gorlosius was still mounted as well, on a wiry stallion with a coat as black as his own hair. What he might lack in brute strength he made up in quickness. No sooner had an enemy focused on him than he was gone. Eldaul, on the other hand, was too big a man for most horses. He waded into battle with a sword in each hand, and when one blade shattered, replaced it with an axe he had won from a foe. As he fought his way through the camp the bodies piled up behind him like earth thrown up by the plough.

Then the men who had attacked the ships regrouped at the water's edge and drove those who were trying to escape that way back onto the attackers' swords. The incoming tide ran red above the bloodstained sands.

After that it was soon over. Merlin made his way down the hill. The Frisian, Pascentius, had been killed, and the Irish chieftain, Gillomanus, was captured. But in the battle his leg had been half severed. Even if he were ransomed, he would fight no more against Britannia. Most of the other prisoners were put to the sword.

Merlin moved among their own wounded, cleaning and binding the dreadful gashes, stitching when there was need. Most of these men were scarred already, and they were as healthy as their own ponies. There was good reason to hope they would heal, though he had known a tiny scratch to bring death to a man in his prime. He wondered how Aurelianus had died—for after finding the enemy where he had predicted, he no longer doubted that the first part of his vision was also true. Had some disease stricken the emperor, or had his heart given out at last?

Angry voices roused him from his absorption. He finished securing a bandage and got to his feet. One voice was that of Uthir, clipped and low. The other, louder, belonged to Gorlosius.

"All that those wretches had stolen was on those ships, and you burned them!" exclaimed the Cornovian.

"Would you rather they escaped with it?" Uthir was hanging onto his temper surprisingly well.

"We would have prevented that—" Gorlosius gestured toward the bodies being dragged towards the pyre.

"Perhaps. I had to be sure."

"We should have returned that wealth to its owners, or used it to feed our forces if the owners could not be found. We all bled for this—we deserve a share in the reward!"

"Do you?" Uthir's voice sharpened. "Dumnonia has suffered least of all. If the rest of us can do without, you can afford it as well!"

"Don't use that tone with me!" exclaimed Gorlosius. "You have only the word of this sorcerer that the emperor is dead and yet you are claiming his mantle. Do you think because you're his brother it will automatically go to you? The new High King must be elected from among all the princes when that time comes."

"And so he will be." Uthir's voice shook with the effort he was making to retain control. "But until we return to Venta, the command of this army is mine, and you will obey!"

They took the road south as soon as their wounded could travel. By the time they reached Demetia the messengers had found them. Aurelianus was dead indeed—of illness, said some, while others whispered of poison, though no culprit could be found. The comet had been seen all over the land, and its meaning widely disputed. But by that time, one of Uthir's men had made a banner bearing a red dragon, its head haloed in light. *Pendragon*, "Dragonhead," they hailed him, and the word ran ahead of them so that by the time they reached Venta Belgarum, the whole countryside was calling him by that name.

And it was as Uthir Pendragon that the princes of Britannia hailed him as their High King.

VII

A HERITAGE OF POWER

A.D. 461

THE HOUSE OF THE HIGH PRIESTESS SMELLED OF SICKNESS. AFTER THE fresh breeze off the lake, it was almost overpowering. Igierne stopped short in the entry, summoning her self-control, and little Morgause bumped into her. The message had said that Argantel was ill and wanted her, but the figure in the bed seemed shrunken, and even the lamplight could not lend a healthy color to her skin. The old woman who sat by her stood up and motioned to them to enter; Igierne recognized Ebrdila, who had served as Argantel's deputy when the High Priestess was away.

Igierne grasped the child's shoulder, holding her tightly, and Morgause, who could never bear to be restrained, struggled to get free.

"Your grandmother is resting, little one—" With an effort she kept her voice steady. "Why don't you run down to the shore to play?"

She felt the girl shake her head. "I want to kiss her."

Igierne looked down at Morgause's ruddy curls with the exasperation her daughter so often aroused in her. This was not how she wished the child to remember her grandmother, but Morgause was almost six, old enough to face the reality of death. With a sigh she released her grip, and followed her inside.

"Mother—"

Argantel's eyelids quivered. For a moment she gazed unseeing, then the blue eyes focused and she smiled. Her hair had just begun to gray before Amlodius died; it was white now. Igierne swallowed. Her parents had always been so matter-of-fact about their marriage. Who would have thought that losing her husband would blight Argantel's autumnal splendor?

"You came . . . and the little one too. . . . It is well that you had a daughter first . . . to inherit . . . the trust."

"I'm not ready," said Igierne.

"Neither was I. . . . Your path lies still in the world . . ." Argantel reached out and grasped her daughter's hand. "You must go back, and be Tigernissa. But a time will come when you will return to be the Lady of the Lake on this Isle. And this one . . . shall rule after you. . . ." She reached out to the child.

Was that a curse, wondered Igierne, or a promise? Morgause's dark eyes grew round, then she bent and kissed the old woman's papery cheek.

"Grandmother, are you a queen?"

Argantel smiled. "In a way I am. . . . Remember, whatever happens in the outer world, so long as the Lady of the Lake . . . rules here . . ." she paused, fighting for breath, "the Goddess still lives . . . in Britannia."

"Not in the South," Igierne said bitterly. "The bishops preach against the old festivals, or change their meaning, and call woman the root of evil. The Saxons are pagans, therefore no loyal Briton can honor our ancient gods!"

"That's enough," said Ebrdila. "You are tiring her." Igierne remembered her mother telling her that the older woman had wanted to be High Priestess once. But she seemed honestly grief-stricken now.

Argantel's features twisted in a grimace that was trying to be a smile. "Let me talk. . . . I will be quiet soon."

"Cannot you do something?" Igierne asked Ebrdila. "You know all the secrets of healing here! Cannot the power of the Cauldron make her whole?" She did not speak of the Sword. Its power was of another kind.

Ebrdila drew herself up. "Do you understand so little? The Hallows can set aright only that which counters the way of nature. But even the Cauldron cannot mend a heart which is outworn!"

Argantel shook her head. "Truly, daughter, if you had not been here, I do not think I would have lived so long. . . . Do not waste the time I have left in mourning. You may weep when I am gone."

Igierne bit her lip and looked down. Morgause had slipped away from the bedside and was wandering about the chamber, fingering the hangings and carved beams, the vessels of silver and bronze, all the odd bits of paraphernalia that had accumulated there.

"You have borne your daughter for the Lake. Now you must bear a son for Britannia."

"How? It has been months since Gorlosius sought my bed. But I was married by Christian rites. I cannot divorce him."

"Gorlosius will not . . . father your child."

"Who, then?"

"You will know. . . ." Argantel's smile faded. "But you must not fail . . . in your trust. Guard the Sword until your son is a man!"

Igierne stared into her mother's blue eyes that were so like her own. Argantel's fingers twitched anxiously, and Ebrdila lifted her hand and set it on her daughter's head.

"Witness!" whispered the High Priestess. "To Igierne I pass the power! May the gods of our people bear witness to what I say!"

She fell back and lay gasping, but Igierne swayed and nearly fell, dizzied by the pulse of energy, as if her mother's life had passed into her through her hand.

"Go. She will sleep now. I will call you if there is need."

There was command in Ebrdila's voice, and Igierne rose,

looking down at her mother's closed face. She wanted to throw her arms around her, weeping, but Argantel was already leaving her. She bowed her head and turned, and as she did so, Ebrdila also stood, and made her the obeisance due a High Priestess, or a queen.

That night, after Morgause had been put to bed, Igierne walked upon the shore. A little after Igierne had left her, Argantel had slipped into sleep as well, a slumber from which she could not be wakened. From the house of the High Priestess Igierne could hear singing as the women of the Isle of Maidens chanted the verses that guide a departing spirit home.

The past few days had been cloudy, but tonight the sky was clear, and the quiet waters of the lake glittered with reflected stars. As she gazed, light seemed to blossom beneath the waters. She looked up and saw the comet, hanging like a firedrake in the sky.

For a long time she watched it, her heart wrenched between anguish and exaltation. When at last she sought her bed, she dreamed of a battle on the sands. In the chill hour just before sunrise, Ebrdila woke her to say that her mother was gone.

Londinium was hot and crowded and full of bad smells. The only thing it did not have in overabundance, thought Igierne, was Saxons. Riding through the empty lands along the Tamesis, she had longed for the safety of the Lake. Now she longed for its peace. Her horse snorted and tried to rear as a peddler waved a tray of glass bangles almost under its nose. She reined the beast down, glancing at her husband in irritation.

"If you were going to ask me again to allow you to return to the Isle of Maidens," said Gorlosius, "the answer is still no. I gave you leave to attend your mother's deathbed, not to become the High Priestess of a pagan cult. You will not speak of that while we are in Londinium, do you understand? The princes will not choose a man who would bring them a pagan queen!"

Since the death of his father, she thought angrily, he had become even more autocratic.

"Do you think my silence will make any difference?" asked Igierne. "They all know who I am. I thought it was for an alliance with the powers of the North that you married me."

"The *secular* power of the North," he snapped in reply. "And you should not have left my daughter on the Isle."

"Your message commanded my presence at your side," she answered sweetly. "It said nothing of Morgause."

"Well, that is past praying for now, and perhaps it will do no harm. Until she reaches an age for marriage no one will care too much where a girl-child is bestowed."

"I wonder that you men have not found some other method of begetting offspring if you consider females of such little worth."

Gorlosius refused to dignify that sally with an answer. The old governor's palace was before them; the warriors guarding the gate straightened to attention as the Cornovian prince rode in, and returned Igierne's smile. It was not their fault that her husband had ordered her to join him, she thought as they continued across the inner courtyard. And she might need friends one day.

The basilica of Londinium was the largest building Igierne had ever seen, and drafty. It was a place for court and council, and so it remained. The altar which had once received incense for the emperor had been taken down, but the flaking portraits of dead Caesars still watched from the walls. In Byzantium, she had heard, the emperor was still treated as if he were a god. She sighed as she watched the gesticulating figures below from her place with the other wives. Things were different in Britannia.

"There was a time," Eleutherius of Eburacum was saying as he addressed the other princes, "when our numbers would have been too many even for this hall! Too many of our men of good family have gone to Armorica. It is those of us who have remained, standing fast against the enemy, who should rule, not a man whose family fled."

"Nonsense!" Uthir answered him. "Half the lords of Dumnonia and Demetia rule more lands in lesser Britannia than they do here. My father never ran from the Saxons; my brother and I went only to avoid weakening this island by civil war. And when Britannia called we came back again. *You* summoned the 'sons of Ambrosius' to come and lead you—not Aurelianus alone. You've already chosen me!"

He had not raised his voice, but it carried clearly. He was too far away for Igierne to make out his features, but she wondered if the relaxed lines of his body represented unconcern or an exquisite control.

The woman sitting beside her leaned closer. "He only says the truth. And they say his soldiers love him. If he went outside and appealed to the men, they would raise him on their shields as emperors were made in the old days."

Why was it only the men who were deciding? wondered Igierne. The Saxons killed women as well as warriors. It was said, of course, that a woman influenced the outcome by influencing her husband, but to Gorlosius, she was only a symbol of his status, like the golden torque he wore. Her father, she remembered, had valued her mother's wisdom. In that moment she missed them both acutely. How foolish she had been to expect that her own marriage would be the same.

"Your husband is not a candidate, then?" asked Igierne.

"Oh no. He is Caius Turpilius, a gentleman of good family, but no prince. I am Flavia. But Uthir will have his vote. My husband has served with the prince through several campaigns."

"So has mine," answered Igierne dryly. "But I think I would rather have Uthir as High King."

Flavia, once she had started talking, seemed eager to be friendly. Igierne learned in short order that she had a young son at home and would like more children, but feared it was not to be, for the child was large, and the birth had been a hard one.

"A fine strapping boy is my Cai, but it's hard to bear sons, knowing that as soon as they can hold a blade they'll be off to war. I could almost wish he had been a girl."

"Girls can be a trial too," said Igierne, remembering how Morgause had wept when she rode away. But she was more certain than ever that she had been wise to leave the girl safe in the North.

Eldaul of Glevum was speaking now. His connection with Vitalinus gave him a claim, but was also his greatest liability. Fortunately he seemed to be without ambition, and was supporting his commander.

"Do you think the Protector of Eburacum a serious contender?" asked Flavia.

"He would like to be, but he is young and untried," answered Igierne dispassionately. "The same goes for Agricola of Demetia, and Honorius. Many of the men who might have been contenders died at Sorviodunum. Northerners from beyond the Wall, like Ridarchus, are too far away to be considered, though they make useful allies. I hope that they will choose Uthir."

"You know a great deal about it—" said Flavia.

"Really? You would never think it, to hear my husband. . . ."

Flavia followed the direction of her gaze and understanding dawned suddenly. "You don't want to be queen?"

"I don't particularly want Gorlosius to be High King," Igierne replied.

Flavia raised one eyebrow, then her eyes widened. "And who in the name of Christ and His holy mother is *that*?"

She pointed, and Igierne saw a tall figure that appeared to have formed itself from the shadows behind Uthir. A singularly inappropriate invocation, thought Igierne, recognizing, even at this distance, the slightly stooping posture and the dark hair. But he had changed; his finery had been replaced by a plain white robe and his beard swept his chest. As if he had felt her gaze upon him, he looked up, eyes fierce as a hawk's beneath heavy brows.

"That is my cousin," she said softly, "Merlin. . . ."

* * *

She did not encounter Merlin again until the Council was over and the princes and their wives gathered at the church to see Uthir anointed and crowned. Despite the arguments, the choice had been, she thought, inevitable. The Pendragon's name was on every tongue. If the princes had chosen another ruler, no one would have followed him.

During the Council, Igierne had come to value Flavia's simple friendliness. They stood together now outside the little church, mantles wrapped tightly, for a damp wind had come up, promising rain. With the other women and less important chieftains they waited for the princes to emerge, for the little church could not hold them all. Merlin stood apart, appearing rather monkish himself in his white robe. But from what she had heard, he was no longer any kind of Christian at all. From time to time she would find him watching her, but when their eyes met he looked away.

Before we leave here I will find time to talk to him, she thought, *even if Gorlosius disapproves.*

If the bishop sealed the rite by offering communion she wondered if her husband would receive it. It was a sin, she had been told, to take the sacrament when one's heart was full of anger or envy, and Gorlosius had been festering with fury since the decision was made. She listened with half an ear to Flavia chatter about her eagerness to get back to her child and her home, reflecting that this was what a marriage should be.

I will go home to Dun Tagell with Gorlosius, she told herself, *but when he goes off to fight again, I will leave as well. The Lady of the Lake should not be at any man's beck and call.*

The church doors swung open. From inside came a wave of incense and the sound of voices joined in song. Men began to come out of the sanctuary, blinking in the light. A murmur of anticipation spread through the crowd.

"The Pendragon! The High King comes!"

Igierne felt a wave of dizziness and took a deep breath. Interesting, she thought—his brother had been addressed as emperor, but Uthir obviously favored a British title, accepting that the Roman days were done. More men emerged, a guard of honor, who stood away to either side, drawing their swords. She moved back a little and felt a hand grasp her elbow. It was Merlin.

"You must stay here until they come. . . ."

Before she could ask why, color blazed at the church door. The bishop was coming through, clad in his embroidered cope, and beside him, his brow bound with gold and his shoulders draped in a purple mantle that flowed over a white garment like a priest's gown, came the king.

He looked dazed, thought Igierne, and not because the sun was coming out at last. His gaze was the rapt stare of one who has looked on a holy thing. Two priests guided him between the lines of warriors; he blinked and lifted a hand to acknowledge the cheers.

The crowd surged toward him, shouting, but somehow Merlin was in front of them, still holding Igierne by the arm.

"All hail to the Pendragon of Britannia—" said Merlin. Igierne knew that the people were still shouting, but the noise was muted, as if the three of them stood within a bubble that shut out sound. "I bring you the blessing of the ancient powers, and I bring you the White Raven, the hidden queen!"

Slowly, Uthir's gaze moved from Merlin to Igierne. What was he seeing? She had cast back her hood when the sun came out and with it her veil; she could feel the sun warm on her hair. She felt herself flushing as the dazed wonder in his face became a very focused awe.

Abruptly she understood that he was seeing not an ordinary woman, the wife of one of his chieftains, but the Goddess in mortal form. And understanding, her own awareness became that of the priestess, and looking upon him, she saw not Uthir the man, but the King.

It was Gorlosius who broke the spell.

"Come away, woman!" He took her arm and pulled her after him. "And put on your veil. Our great king has better things to do than stare at you!"

They turned a corner and he let her go, glaring. "What did Uthir say to you?"

Igierne straightened her mantle and drew her veil back over her hair. "He said nothing. Nothing at all," she said coldly.

He had not needed to, she thought as she turned and began to walk toward their lodgings. As king and queen their spirits had touched, and she could not predict what was going to happen now.

Igierne had been taught that the six weeks before the equinox were a time of change, in both the inner worlds and the lands of men. True it was that no sooner had she and Gorlosius arrived at Dun Tagell than the weather grew stormy. From then until the autumnal equinox, the outer coasts of Dumnonia were lashed by violent weather, but the conflicts in the skies were only a mild reflection of the tumults in the affairs of men.

For Gorlosius, overriding by sheer force of will his father's old councilors, had declared Dumnonia a kingdom separate from Britannia, and renounced his oaths to the High King. The rock of Dun Tagell, which had known peace since Vitalinus brought the Cornovii down from the north to drive the men of Eriu away, became a garrison.

The Latin name for the place was Durocornovium, the stronghold of the Cornovii. Its defenses were limited to a wall that enclosed a hall and a barracks built of the native stone, but it needed no more, for it was set on an outcrop at the edge of the sea, with only a narrow bridge of rock to link it to the land. It was not clear to Igierne whether her husband had settled her there to hold it for him, or whether the dozen men assigned to it were there to keep watch on her. Gorlosius himself paid her only an occasional visit. Isca Dumnoniorum and Durnovaria were the first lines of his defense, and to her relief he had little time for his western holdings.

From time to time word came to them of the progress of the war. The new High King, desperate to settle the situation before the Saxons could organize themselves to take advantage of British disunity, had struck swiftly and hard. Gorlosius had fallen back from Durnovaria and made a new frontier at Isca, but Uthir, seeking to besiege him in the city, left a back way open, and instead of driving his enemy down toward Belerion in the toe of the peninsula, had allowed him to escape toward the western coast where Gorlosius had hopes of joining with allies from Eriu.

By the time Uthir caught up with him his enemy had gone to ground once more in an ancient hill-fort called Dimilioc, a few miles south of Dun Tagell. And there they held, as the cold winds blew and the nights lengthened toward winter, until the feast of Samhain, when the dead come home.

Torchflames flickered wildly in the draft, chasing shadows like fleeing bogles into the corners of the hall. Try though they might, thought Igierne, they could never make the building completely proof against the wind. Always before, she had spent the winter in the villa above the sheltered waters of the Fawwyth, on the protected southern coast of Cornovia. In the summer Dun Tagell could be delightful, with the gulls calling as they wheeled above and the sunlight sparkling on the waves. But it was a cold and damp and dismal place to spend the wintertime!

With a silent curse for the husband who had left her here, Igierne set the basket of apples, last of the summer's store, up on the table. It was a poor feast—if they had any sense, those spirits to whom it was offered would return to some table that was better supplied. If there were enough, she reflected, frowning, to go around. In these past years so many had died, and so many of the families who did survive had fled the land. Any ancestors who sought them would have a long way to go.

And so she set out the fruit and the barley bread, and the dishes of boiled meat and cheese. And despite the draft, she fixed the great doorway just a little ajar so that any spirit that might wish to share the hospitality of Dun Tagell could come in.

Certainly the men of her garrison appreciated the break in the monotony of their duty. There was no mead, but when she brought round the ale pitcher they grinned and held out their cups. The drinking went on until late, for there were many toasts to be made, to comrades lost in the recent fighting, to her mother, and to Aurelianus, who lay now in the barrow beside the Giant's Dance with the lords whom Hengest had slain.

By the evening's ending, sorrow had been translated to melancholy on a golden tide of ale. The men went singing to their barracks, and even Igierne's two women were nodding. She herself had drunk enough to feel an unaccustomed detachment, but she was not yet sleepy. When she had helped her women to their beds, she eased out the door and climbed carefully to the lookout post on the wall.

A three-quarter moon glimmered between tattered clouds, touching an occasional glint of silver from the restless waves. And from time to time the water would catch a flicker of light from the torches that burned on the walls, as if the people of the sea were celebrating their own festival. Lights had been kindled over the gates, and at the other end of the arching causeway, to aid any spirit that might be uncertain of the road in finding its way.

Though surely, she thought as she gazed at the shadowed masses of the cliffs beyond it, any spirit that could find a path between the worlds could manage to travel this last little way. She blinked—for a moment she had thought she saw something moving—but when she looked again the land was as dark and featureless as before.

It is the ale, she thought, shaking her head. *I had best seek my bed before I try to walk the moonpath across the sea.*

She made her way down from the wall, choosing her footing with conscious care. The hall seemed warm after the brisk wind outside, and she cast aside her shawl. The pitcher still stood upon the table, half full of ale. It would be flat by morning, and it seemed a pity to waste it when there were so many dead whom she had not yet honored. She filled her cup and raised it high.

"To Amlodius, shield of the North!"

She had barely begun the tally of her father's dead companions when the lamplight flickered wildly and a gust of wind stirred her hair. She looked up. The door to the hall had swung open; three figures were standing there.

"Be you living or dead, I give you greeting—" She held out the beaker. "In the name of the old gods and the new, be welcome to this hall."

They came forward, and the third man closed the door behind them. Igierne blinked, thinking she must have drunk more than she thought, for she found it hard to focus on their features. Then the leader stopped before her and held out his hand to take the cup. He was wearing a checkered mantle she knew only too well, with a golden griffin pin.

"Gorlosius!" she exclaimed, almost dropping the cup. "What are you doing here?"

For a moment he hesitated. "Where else should I be on this holy festival?" His voice seemed strained and hoarse, as if he were very tired. "I gave my army the slip and came here. I couldn't go any longer without seeing you again."

Igierne took a step back and snatched up the lamp, but his features were still in shadow.

"You come here on Samhain Eve, like a spirit from the Otherworld, and you expect me to welcome you?"

"Is it so strange to expect a wife to welcome her husband?"

"It is when I am the wife," she said with a bitter humor, "and the husband is you."

One of his men—she thought his name was Jordanus—hovered anxiously behind him. The third man kept to the shadows by the door. Perhaps they were spirits, she thought, her skin prickling, for surely this was not the Gorlosius she had known.

"Nonetheless," he said harshly, "this night I'll claim a husband's place in your bed!" Before she could react he was beside her, gripping her shoulders with a warrior's callused hands.

But not the hands of Gorlosius. He was a living man—so close, she could feel the warmth of his body; her nostrils flared to the scents of sweat and horse—but her flesh knew that this man had never touched her before.

"I am the Lady of the Lake," she said in a still voice, "and not to be deceived by lesser magics. In the name of the gods my people swear by I conjure your true form back again."

Whether the change was in him or in herself she could not say, but the air seemed to ripple around him, and when it cleared she was looking up into the face of the High King.

"Why?" she said softly. "Why have you sought to dishonor me?"

Uthir shook his head. "The disguise was to protect you. The man at the gate thought I was Gorlosius, and let me in."

"I asked the wrong question," Igierne said then. "Why have you tried to deceive me? It is not the way of a lover to court in the guise of another man, nor is it the way of a king."

"It is the way of a desperate man . . ." he whispered then, glancing toward the man by the door in appeal.

"What is that to me?" exclaimed Igierne. She was slow to wrath, but she was growing angry now. "If this is love, it can learn to wait; if it is lust, then burn!"

"This is the hour in which the Pendragon is destined to beget his son," said the third man, coming at last into the light. "The child which you conceive in this hour, and no other, shall be the Defender of Britannia."

"Merlin . . ." she breathed, remembering how she had faced him across the altar of the Sword. "Is this truly so?"

He bowed his head. "I have seen it in the heavens."

"I will not be coerced . . . even by the stars. . . ."

Uthir stared at her, his desperation gradually giving way to the awe with which he had looked upon her as he came from his crowning.

"Lady—I won't force you." Taking a deep breath, he got down upon one knee. "You are the White Raven of Britannia; you decide." He took her hand and gently kissed the palm.

At the touch of his lips a little shock traveled up her arm. She bit her lip, feeling a warmth spreading through her despite the chill air. She held out her other hand, and trembled as he kissed it.

"You are so beautiful, Igierne," he said softly. "You haunt my sleep, and I dream you are my queen."

"Truly?" She laughed suddenly, her anger giving way to a fierce exhilaration. "Then as a queen I will claim you! You shall come to my bed, and we will see what ancient soul is hovering in these shadows, waiting to take flesh in my womb!"

One end of the hall had been partitioned off with curtains and woven screens to give the master of the fortress some privacy. A few swift steps brought her to the entrance. Uthir surged to his feet and followed her.

In the dim light that came through the curtain she saw him in silhouette, stripping off his mantle and heavy outer tunic, struggling with the buckles of his commander's belt, and finally letting it drop with a clatter to the floor. She unhooked belt and brooches, pulling first the short-sleeved outer garment and then the long-sleeved undertunic over her head so that she stood shivering in her shift before him.

He had got as far as his braes. Her eyes had adjusted to the dim light, and her breath caught as she took in his breadth of shoulder and the fine modeling of muscle in belly and arm. She knelt to unknot his leg wrappings and he bent, plucking the pins from her coiled hair so that it fell in silken masses about her shoulders.

"Lie down," he whispered. "If you touch me now I will waste the good seed."

She pulled away, looking up at him, and saw that it was true. She wanted to laugh, but her pulse was leaping erratically, and she realized that she had come already to a state of readiness that Gorlosius, with all his efforts, had rarely been able to bring her. She tugged at the neck ties of her shift and as she rose it slid off her shoulders and pooled around her feet. She padded to the bed and lay down upon it, clad only in her hair.

For one moment longer Uthir hesitated, then he surrendered himself to her embrace, and as the embers flare when new fuel is thrust into the hearth, their bodies caught fire. With arms and legs she held fast as the flames rose higher. Then they exploded in a shower of light, brilliant behind her closed eye-lids, and he cried out and arched hard against her and then fell like a slain man back into her arms.

For a few moments they lay gasping. Then Igierne ran her hands down the rippling muscles of his back and felt him come to life again between her thighs. This time their joining had a sweet deliberation that left her panting and helpless in his arms. They made love a third time before they slept, but long afterward, when she thought about that night, it seemed to her that it must have been in the first encounter that she got her son, when all the High King's hoarded passion was released in that great cry.

She felt Uthir's contentment change to the relaxation of sleep, and had time only to draw the blankets over them before oblivion claimed her as well. It was some hours later that she awakened, wondering what had disturbed her, for Uthir lay still beside her and there had been no sound. She opened her eyes, abruptly certain they were not alone.

Beside the curtains a pale shape moved.

She blinked, remembering how a trick of the light on the bedcurtains had been able to frighten her when she was a child. But this image grew ever more distinct until she could make out the tense, wiry shape beneath the mantle, the shock of dark hair and staring eyes. Spectral lips shaped her name.

"Gorlosius . . ." she whispered, answering.

The shape reached towards her. Then from the pen beside the garden came a cock's crow, and its features contorted and began to fade.

Was it Gorlosius's spirit body or his shade? Igierne lay trembling until in the gray hour just after dawn, when the mist lies heavy on the sea, the stillness was broken by someone shouting. She heard the door to the hall slam open and sat up, pulling the blanket around her, as Uthir began to stir by her side.

"My lady, my lady! The High King's men have stormed the fort and struck down Gorlosius. Come quickly, and we will help you to flee!"

The curtains were flung back. She saw two of her husband's

men, their armor bloodied, their frantic faces stiffening to astonishment as the torchlight showed them who was sitting there. For a moment Igierne's mind went blank with terror. Then the warrior went down on one knee.

"Lord Gorlosius, I saw you fall!"

"I escaped," said Uthir. As a commander, Igierne thought numbly, he must have developed the ability to sound sensible moments after being awakened by an alarm.

"Then you must flee again, for the Pendragon will surely come here to secure this stronghold!"

"If he's taken Dimilioc then my cause is lost, and I must make peace with him. Go back—tell the men to lay down their arms. The High King won't condemn them for following their prince!"

"Aye, my lord—" said the warrior, sorrow replacing the terror in his eyes. He regained his feet and pushed back out through the curtains.

Igierne let out her pent breath in a long sigh.

Uthir was already pulling on his clothing. "What a tangle—" he muttered. "But with all the rumors that will fly, I suppose no one will know what's true!" He belted his tunic and reached for the checkered mantle.

Igierne still sat with the blanket around her shoulders, watching him. "Does anyone know that?" she said softly.

He stilled, and the warmth came back into his eyes. A swift step brought him to her side and he kissed her.

"I know that you're my queen! Bar the gates after me; and don't let anyone in until I come for you!"

It seemed very quiet when he had gone.

I am a widow . . . thought Igierne, remembering Gorlosius's anguished ghost. Then, deliberately, she thrust the memory away. *I am a queen*, she told herself, and set her hands above her belly, where even now the future Defender of Britannia, planted in her womb like a seed of light, was beginning to glow.

VIII

THE SIGN OF THE BEAR

A·D· 471

"MORGAUSE, YOUR HAIR IS LIKE MY MOTHER'S, THE WAY IT WAS when I was a child," said Igierne, drawing the comb through the long strands. "It shines like a dark fire."

Through the narrow window of the tower a thin spring sunlight glowed on rich fabric, sparkled from the jewelry waiting in its casket, and struck fiery glints from the girl's long hair. Once, this had been part of the Roman fortress of Eburacum, but Coelius had made it a royal residence. Now his son Eleutherius ruled, and seemed happy to host the wedding of his overlord's daughter to Leudonus of Dun Eidyn.

Morgause shrugged as if she were not convinced, but she stood still as her mother took up the next strand and began to tease the snarls free. Poor child, thought Igierne, at fifteen her hair was almost her only beauty. She herself had been the same at her first marriage, a pudgy adolescent with no graces to charm her new husband. She wished they could have delayed this wedding until Morgause grew into her own looks, but Uthir needed the northern alliance now. She could only hope that Leudonus would have the sensitivity to cherish this flower until it bloomed. Now in his thirties, he had buried one wife already, and was newly come to his grandfather's throne.

She finished the last lock and smoothed it into place. "There now. Put on the jewels and you will look splendid!" She picked up the necklet of Alban gold.

"I look terrible," said Morgause. "I hate this color—"

"Crimson is traditional," Igierne began, although she had to agree that this particular shade did not flatter her daughter's complexion.

"—and I hate this city. You should have left me on the Isle of Maidens to finish my training. The Isle needs a High Priestess, and if you do not want the position, I do not see why it should not go to me."

Igierne stared at her. *I do want it*, she thought, and each time she had visited Morgause she had wanted to stay with her. But Uthir needed her, and when she was with him, her memories of the Lake became a fair dream.

"Perhaps one day it will," she said aloud. "But the Lady of the Lake needs to know the ways of the world as well. And we need you here—"

"Then why are you sending me to Dun Eidyn?" retorted Morgause, sliding the bracelets onto her wrists.

"Would you rather we had wedded you to some southern magnate who thinks the old ways are a sin?" exclaimed Igierne. "At least the Votadini still honor the gods. Leudonus's mother was a Pictish princess. He will know how to value you not only as Uthir's daughter, but as my heir."

Morgause looked thoughtful as she hung the discs of gold filigree in her ears, and Igierne was unhappily reminded that the girl was her only heir, so far as the world knew. In ten years of marriage, she had given Uthir no other child than the one tiny son, born six weeks before his time at Dun Tagell, the Midsummer after his conception, and handed over to Merlin to foster as soon as it became clear that he would live. She had given him her mother's family name, Artorius, but she would not even know him if she saw him now.

"Well, at least Leudonus is not a bad-looking man," Morgause said finally, finishing with the second earring. "And, as you keep reminding me, he is a king." As she held up the bronze mirror Igierne saw them both for a moment reflected—

Morgause ruddy with her father's dark eyes, and herself still pale and fair. But the bronze canceled out such differences, revealing the elegant modeling of cheek and brow, the firm line of the jaw, and beyond such surface similarities, their pride.

There was a stir at the doorway. Igierne turned, expecting the women whom she had banished from her chambers, wanting a little time alone with this daughter whom she was about to lose once more. But it was the High King—with Merlin, as usual, behind him.

"Go out now," she said briskly. "The other ladies are waiting with your wreath and veil. In a few moments I will follow you."

Morgause looked from her mother to Uthir with thinly veiled hostility, but she went without arguing.

"I hope this marriage will work," said the king, looking after her.

"That is the chance you take, is it not, when you marry girls off so young, and without consulting their inclination," Igierne replied, a bit more sharply than she had intended. "What's to say they won't find someone that suits them better when they are grown?"

Uthir had the grace to flush, and her frown softened. Since their marriage he had put on flesh, and from time to time he experienced episodes of dizziness and joint pain that worried her, but he still looked at her with the ardent gaze that had won her ten years ago. With Uthir she had the kind of partnership she had dreamed of, and their physical harmony had only increased with the years.

"It will be enough if Leudonus is as brisk in bed as he is in battle, since her children may be my heirs . . ." he said thoughtfully.

"But what about our son? Isn't it time you brought him to court and acknowledged him? How can he be a king if he is not trained up to rule?"

"How can he be a king if he's dead?" Uthir responded. "People tried to poison my brother and me three times before we were fifteen. Aurelianus never did get over it, really. And we were Ambrosius's legitimate sons!"

"Are you saying that Artorius is not?" Her voice shook.

"Not by Church law—we weren't married 'til Midwinter. A pity the child came early. Curse it, I myself proved how Gorlosius could have visited you six weeks before. The boy's too young to face the whispers that will follow once I claim him. People know you bore me a child, but many think he died, and they don't know where he is now. He is safe, Igierne; let him be!"

"Is he?" Igierne whispered. She turned to Merlin. "He was such a tiny mite when you took him away from me. Have you told me the truth, cousin? Did he live and thrive, or is he only a few tiny bones in an unmarked grave?" It was a nightmare that haunted her—that Gorlosius's ghost had somehow blighted Uthir's seed.

"On your mother's soul I swear, I have seen him every year since he was born," Merlin said quietly.

"Have you seen him this year?" she exclaimed. "You made me Tigernissa, and as High Queen I command you. Go to him, Merlin, and report to me every detail of how he looks and what he does! Then, perhaps, I will believe."

Over her head the two men exchanged a look. Then Merlin nodded. Igierne knew they were humoring her. Perhaps it was seeing Morgause again that made her so desperate to know about her son.

"I will go to him," said the druid, "as soon as the marriage festivities are done."

She drew a trembling breath. "The wedding procession will be forming. You must take your places. Give me a moment to compose myself, and I will come."

On the table there was a flagon with wine. She poured some into a goblet and drank, waiting for her breathing to slow. There was a sound from the entry and she turned. Morgause was standing there, with two spots of color blazing in her cheeks. How long had she been there? wondered her mother. What had she heard?

"It's *him*—it's my brother that you really want, isn't it?" the girl said in a low voice. "But he doesn't even know who you are, and Ebrdila was more of a mother to me than you. You might as well never have had any children at all! If I have babies I swear I will keep them by me! They, at least, will know they had their mother's love!"

She turned in a swirl of draperies and swept out.

After a moment Igierne's fury turned to a laughter that edged hysteria. She gulped down the rest of the wine and strove to control her breathing. It seemed a long time before she was calm once more. But when she emerged at last, the wedding procession was just getting underway. She took her husband's arm, and the High King and High Queen of Britannia escorted Morgause to meet her destiny.

Always, when Merlin came into the pleasant lands above the Sabrina estuary, he felt he was moving back in time. The Silure tribesmen to whom they had once belonged had long ago embraced the manners and culture of Rome, and though the old tribal capital of Venta Silurum now went by the name of Ker-Venta, on Saturday evenings the gentlemen of the countryside heated their baths, and they rode to visit, in the old fashion, in a carriage and pair.

Merlin traveled on a sturdy gray mule, and he preferred to lie upon a patch of woodland rather than seek shelter with folk he did not know, and to bathe in the cold stream. The silence of the forest eased his spirit, and he blessed Igierne for sending him on this errand. Caius and Flavia would be surprised to see him, but their son Cai and Artor their fosterling knew him only as a wandering druid, and accepted his comings and goings without questioning.

He came to the villa a week before the old festival of the goddess of the harvest and Lugos her defender at the time when the grain begins to ripen in the fields, which the Christians now called the Feast of Mary. To the people it made little difference; as always, they prepared to offer their first fruits to the Lady, and pray to the Lord to protect the harvest. It was not only the wheat that was growing stiff and golden and the barley heads that were beginning to hang low. In the orchards, the topmost apples were blushing red and golden with promise of sweetness to come.

As Merlin turned down the lane from the High Road the branches of one of the trees began to shiver as if agitated by an extremely localized storm. From within the tree came high-pitched shouting. The druid reined in, and after a moment's reflection, spun around himself the sphere of shadow that kept him from being seen.

The branches thrashed again and a small, copper-haired figure dropped to the ground. Merlin recognized him as one of the villa's Irish slaves.

"I can't get them, Cai, no matter how hard I shake. Those apples may look ripe, but they aren't!"

"I have sworn to offer them to Our Lady tomorrow!" said the boy who was standing by the trunk of the tree. Big-boned and black-haired, he had the look of Caius Turpilius senior already. "Climb back up and pick them if they will not fall."

"The top branches are too little—they will break, and I will fall!" objected the slave.

"Well, I am certainly too big to climb up there!" said Cai rather smugly. "Try again! I order you!"

"No," put in the third boy, younger and smaller than the other two. His hair was the color of the tree trunk and he seemed nondescript, until you looked at his eyes. "That is an unjust order, and he doesn't have to obey."

"Be quiet, Artor! I am the master's son, and you are only a nameless fosterling! Treni, get up that tree!"

Merlin bit his lip with remembered pain at the old insult. No doubt Caius Turpilius had kept his promise to raise the child as his own, but boys were acutely sensitive to questions of status; they should have anticipated that the other children would mock Artor.

The boy himself did not change expression. Perhaps he was used to it or perhaps, like Merlin, he had become an expert at hiding his wounds.

Cai gripped the slave's arm and dragged him forward, but before they reached the tree, Artor scrambled up the trunk and gained the lowest branch.

"I'll do it—I'm the lightest of us three. Lie down, Cai, so I can land on something soft if I fall!" A sudden grin transformed his rather stiff expression into a look that caught at the heart. The branches shook as he clambered upward.

Merlin nudged his mule forward, rehearsing spells to knit broken limbs. He could see the topmost branches, and as the Irish boy had stated, they were indeed very thin and small. For a few moments the motion ceased. Had Artor decided not to try it after all? A little way down from the crown of the tree he could see a thickening that might be the boy.

Then something poked up through the leaves. It was a branch, with a twig pointing down like a shepherd's crook. In another moment the branch on which the apple hung was hooked and pulled down into the leaves. *He thinks!* thought Merlin. *He thinks as well as feels.*

"Throw it down, Artor!" came Cai's voice from below. "I'll catch it!"

"You couldn't catch the sun if it fell from the sky," Artor called mockingly. "The apples shall come safe in my tunic, one each for the Virgin, the Mother, and the One who sorrows." Another branch was captured and its fruit disappeared. A third apple went the way of the first two, then the hooked branch dropped and the tree began to shake as the boy started down.

Merlin, who had brought the mule up behind the other two, let out his breath in a long sigh, dropping his concealment, as Artor appeared beneath the leaves and slid to the ground. The boy's gaze traveled past Cai to Merlin and his eyes widened.

"Lord Ambros! Cai—look, the druid has come! Treni, run back to the house and tell Lady Flavia! My lord, we did not expect you until autumn—you've never been here in the summertime!"

He took one of the mule's reins, and Cai took the other, and so escorted, Merlin passed through the orchard and up to the villa where Flavia was waiting.

"You've not come to take him away?" Caius Turpilius asked as they waited for the evening meal. The long porch of the villa faced westward, so they could watch the sun set above the hills.

"Not yet," answered Merlin. "He looks healthy. He is doing well at his studies?"

"Well enough," Caius smiled, "though it is hard to keep the boys to their books on these summer days. His tutor says he asks too many questions."

"And physical exercise?" Merlin already knew that Artor was nimble, but the boys had sworn him to secrecy.

"Cai is better at swordplay—of course he has the advantage of size. Artor is very quick, though, and no quitter. When he has his growth I think he will do well."

A gong announced the imminence of dinner, and they went in. The Turpilius household dined in the old Roman manner, reclining on couches around a central table. The food was simple, but well prepared: the usual hard-boiled eggs; a dish of lentils with cow-parsnips, seasoned with mint and coriander; fried trout from the river with a sauce of herbs and peas from the garden; and a boiled chicken with honey sauce. Merlin had often eaten worse at the table of the High King.

It was more than enough for five adults, for Caius had invited their nearest neighbors as well. Caius and Flavia, of course, knew who and what Merlin was. To their household and neighbors he was merely Ambros, a wandering druid always welcome for his news and his wisdom.

Tonight, they wanted to hear about the wedding. It was surprising, they thought, that the betrothal had not been longer. But perhaps, commented Caius, the High King wanted to secure his northern borders in case Hengest's son Octha returned from Germania.

"What were they about to let him escape?" asked Flavia.

"Because the old wolf had lost his teeth, did they think the young one had no fangs?"

Hengest still lived and held his lands in Cantium, but he had not stirred outside his borders in many a year. No one knew whether he was still the leader of the invasion, or barely holding his own. When they were not attacking the British, a new generation of heathens squabbled with each other, and Octha, who had nearly overrun Eburacum some years before, had been among the most successful.

But after several defeats, Uthir had taken him captive, and instead of killing him outright, as many advised, had held him as a hostage.

"Did they think that Brannos's ravens would guard him? They say that the heathen devil, Woden, is the lord of ravens. Perhaps his birds proved stronger than those of our ancient king!"

They all laughed, but in truth, Merlin had wondered. As long as men could remember, there had been ravens on the hill by the Tamesis that was called the White Mount. According to the ancient lore, it was there that the head of the divine king, Brannos, had been buried, with the promise that so long as it stayed there Londinium should never fall.

After the other guests had departed, Merlin took Caius aside.

"It is in my mind to take Artor with me into the mountains after the festival. There are things that I can teach him there."

"Very well. I will instruct Phylox to pack his things."

Merlin shook his head. "No baggage. To live off the land is part of the teaching."

They left the villa before dawn, for the hills were farther off than they seemed. To Artor, Merlin said that he needed help to gather the herbs that grew wild there. At first Artor skipped ahead, exclaiming at the first birdsongs, the swift dart of the awakening swallows, the flicker of motion as a fox disappeared into the hedge. But as the sun climbed higher, he settled to an observant silence, imitating the druid's ground-eating stride as well as his shorter legs could manage.

Merlin had hoped that they could talk during the journey. When he had visited before, they had always been surrounded by the folk of the villa, and in planning for this journey he had realized that although he had been acquainted with Artor since his birth, he knew only the bright surface that the boy presented to the world. Was this reticence a natural characteristic, he wondered, or a response to the boy's ambivalent status in Caius's family?

Merlin had spent his life gathering knowledge. Since the Night of the Long Knives, when he had failed so disastrously to see through Hengest's cordial mask, he had devoted himself to the study of men's souls, seeking to understand what lay behind their surfaces as once he had studied the secrets of the sky. Uthir depended on him to reveal the hidden motives of the men around him; it should not take long for him to learn the secrets of one child.

By midafternoon they reached a band of open pasture, studded with limestone outcroppings, and began to search for herbs. In the deeper soil they found self-heal, paired leaves marching up the stem to the long purple flower head. In an ointment with goldenrod it was good for infected wounds. Among the rocks twined the strands of mountain pea with their paired leaves and tiny blue flowers.

"Say a prayer of thanks to the spirit of the plant," said Merlin, "and then dig it up and strip off the tubers that cling to the roots."

"What are they good for?" asked the boy.

"Clean one off and chew on it, and you will see. The druids call this *corma*; it will stave off the pangs of hunger and give you energy."

Artor looked dubious, but he did as Merlin asked. In a moment his face changed, and the druid smiled.

"It tastes good . . . sweet. . . ."

"Save the others—you will need them for our journey."

Artor frowned and gazed back across the banding of grass

and woodland that fell away toward the valley of the Wae, veiled by blue summer haze.

"It is midafternoon," he said thoughtfully. "Shouldn't we be turning back soon?"

"Not yet. Just beyond this ridge there is an oak wood that has other plants I need."

At the edge of the forest they found bilberries and brambles whose fruit was just ripening. Artor began to pluck and eat with a boy's enthusiasm, moving deeper and deeper into the wood. Even Merlin was not immune to their attraction, though the taste brought back memories of his wanderings.

What am I doing? he asked himself. *I carry the blood of the Wild Men, who live on such things, but this boy is all human. Can he survive? What will he learn by starving here?*

"He will learn what you learned," his daimon replied. *"He will learn what he is made of . . . and so will you—"*

It seemed to Merlin that the answer was somewhat ambiguous, but he could get nothing more. Still, in this smiling weather, the boy could come to no harm wandering in the woods for a day or even two, and so he watched the sun dip towards the hilltop and kept silence.

The sudden chill as the sun disappeared brought Artor back to awareness of the passage of time. He straightened, looking at Merlin accusingly. "It will be dark long before we get home!"

"That is true," said the druid. "Perhaps we should make camp here and start back in the morning. It will be an adventure—" He added, as Artor looked dubious, "It is something Cai has never done."

As he had expected, that argument had power, and the boy began to look about him with a new interest.

"But what if we get lost?"

"So long as the sky does not fall and the earth stands solid you cannot be truly lost," said the druid, leading the way down the hill. "Have I not taught you how to observe the sun and judge the lie of the land, and what herbs will serve as food?"

"Where will we sleep?" asked Artor.

"Farther down the hill we'll find water, and the trees will shelter us from the wind. Wrap yourself in your cloak and burrow into the leaves and you will sleep warm."

Artor nodded. "Soldiers camp out like this when they're on campaign."

"Do you want to be a soldier?"

"I have to know how to fight. We all do. My foster-father says that if we British had not forgotten how to be warriors, the Saxons would never have come."

"That's so," said Merlin. "That is why Vitalinus hired Hengest in the first place. He begged the magistrates and the chieftains to raise armies, but they were too accustomed to being defended by Rome."

"That was years and years ago—" Artor looked at him skeptically.

"Ah well," said the druid evasively, "that is what I have heard."

Beneath the trees it was growing dark already. They followed the sound of water until they found a grass-grown mudflat above a little stream.

"Are the Saxons truly devils, as Father Paternus says?" asked Artor as they heaped up bracken for bedding and gathered sticks that the spring floods had lodged against the treetrunks to build a fire.

"There are Saxon slaves in Caius Turpilius's household," answered Merlin. "Are they demons?"

"No . . . but they have been baptized."

"The priests make great claims for that holy water of theirs, but I have never noticed that it stopped any man from doing evil if he saw some great advantage in it, or that its lack prevented men from doing good if that was their will. No doubt those same Saxon devils are loving husbands and fathers when they are at home."

"But this isn't their home!" exclaimed Artor.

"The Wild Men might say the same to you. . . ."

Merlin shut his mouth, wondering why he had said that.

Even his mother, before she died, had managed to persuade herself that her child was the offspring of an angelic visitor. He rubbed his arms, with their telltale covering of hair. He had never spoken to anyone of his time in the forest and what he had learned there.

"Wild Men are a legend . . . aren't they?" Artor gave him an odd look, and Merlin wondered what the boy was seeing in the flickering light of their little fire.

"This whole wide earth is a matter of legend. The water is holy, and the stones, and the fire. The wind whispers tales of times that are gone. Maybe you and I will be legends one day."

Artor laughed, and somewhere within, the druid felt a pang. He had plotted and planned for this boy's birth since he first set his hands upon the Sword of Kings. Only by raising up the Defender could he expiate his failure to avert the massacre at Sorviodunum. Only now, gazing into those clear eyes, did it occur to him to question his right to cast Artor in that role.

His mother had cast *him* in the role of Prophet of Britannia. Did it matter that his childhood would have been even more unhappy if he had grown up in Maridunum? Her words, and the Vor Tigernus's need, had set his feet upon the path, and now he could not choose but follow.

But Artor still had a choice. Igierne wanted to bring him up as a prince, but the dangers that had forced his guardians to raise him in ignorance of his destiny had also protected him from its stresses. Unlike Merlin, Artor had been allowed to be a child before he was forced to become a man.

I will teach him all I can, thought the druid, *but in the end, it is the spirit within him that must seek this fate. He must be allowed to choose.*

But that spirit must be tested. A young raven spent many days clinging to the edge of the nest, stretching and beating his wings against the air. Only if he did so would his wings be strong enough to bear him when his spirit finally compelled him to fly.

"You are a good climber," he said aloud. "Perhaps tomorrow we will find some mistletoe. In the lore of the druids it is called all-heal, and the powdered berries have great power against fever and diseases of the heart. But it must be used sparingly, for like many herbs, in the wrong dose it can be a poison."

As the fire burned down he continued to speak of the herbs of the forest and their lore, and which plants were good for food and where they could be found. Artor's eyelids began to droop, for it had been a strenuous day, and presently he sank down upon his leafy bed.

Merlin rubbed out the remains of the fire, but he did not sleep. The stars pricked through the velvet of the sky and the moon rose, and still he watched over the child.

It was nearing midnight when his senses told him that Artor had passed through the borders of sleep and lay now in the deepest slumber, and he arose. First he stripped off his own clothing and rolled it into a tight bundle to carry, for it would only slow him, and in truth, his own body heat made clothing a formality. Then, murmuring spells to keep the boy dreaming, he lifted him in his arms. Artor was no great burden, for he was small for his age, and Merlin's strength was beyond that of humankind. Moving quietly, the druid bore him away.

His long strides carried him through the forest and into the next valley, over a second ridge and down into woodlands that grew beside another stream that like the first flowed into the Wae, but several miles away. There he found a drift of leaves beneath an oak tree and carefully laid the boy down. Chanting softly, he paced a circle around him and sealed it with a sigil of power.

Then he climbed into the tree and curled his long limbs into a fork where the foliage would prevent him from being easily seen from the ground. His situation did not permit deep slumber, but as the night turned from midnight toward dawn he passed into a state halfway between wakefulness and sleeping, suspended between the earth and the stars.

In that dream his spirit hovered above the clearing. With spirit sight he saw the life-force flow through every tree; each leaf outlined in light. And as he watched, the light grew stronger, resolved itself into forms which his mind interpreted as human as they stepped forth from the trees. Merlin's circle had been meant to repel all evil, but these beings were beyond such considerations, like the land itself. The hazels, the green herbs, even the blades of grass had spirits, and all of them gathered around the sleeping boy.

Were they simply curious, or were they drawn by something within him? As Merlin hovered, wondering, he saw Artor's lifelight pulse, and the spirit of the boy, detaching itself as often happens during dreaming, rose up from his body, connected only by a silver cord. He laughed with delight, seeing those bright beings around him, and they bent—in homage, or in welcome?

The rippling stream made a soft background for the chirring of the crickets as the tree-spirits began to dance. At first Artor simply watched in wonder, but presently they drew him into their round. They continued to dance until the moon disappeared behind the hill. Then, one by one, the bright spirits drifted back to shrub or tree, until only the spirit of the oak remained. She it was who escorted the boy's spirit back to his slumbering body, and then herself merged into the solid trunk of the tree once more.

When Merlin woke, it was a little past dawn, and the pile of leaves that covered Artor was beginning to stir. The druid peered through the branches, watching as the boy sat up, rubbing his eyes. It took him some time to realize that not only was the druid not sleeping on the other side of the fire, but that this clearing and this stream were not the ones beside which he had fallen asleep the night before. Merlin could see the moment when his eyes went still and watchful, count the minutes it took for Artor to decide that though he might be lost, he was in no immediate danger.

He got to his feet, brushing off the leaves, and with an instinctive courtesy whose source his waking mind did not remember, relieved himself against a rock instead of a tree. Then he went to the stream to drink, and stayed there for a time, gazing at the light on the trees.

Good, thought the druid, *he is getting his directions from the angle of the sun.*

Artor had already passed the first test, having neither wept nor run screaming in circles, though his face was rather pale. Now he proceeded to pass another, cutting reeds whose tender inner stems were edible and catching several of the big frogs that hid among them. He gathered tinder and managed to get a spark from his flints to light it, and soon the frogs' legs were sizzling on twigs above the fire. Some rather squishy bilberries from his pouch completed his meal—a better breakfast than the druid was having, still perched in his tree.

Then, when the sun was high enough to cast a good shadow, the boy put out his fire and buried the remains of his meal, rolled up his cloak and tied it across his back. But before he set out he paused, looking around him.

"Green lord of the forest," he whispered, "it is not by my own will that I must pass through your realm. Guard my ways until I come to the lands of men."

From what he remembered of the night, Merlin thought the prayer would be heard. But whether it was or not, he himself, unseen, would keep watch until the boy reached safety. With considerable relief he slipped down from the oak tree as Artor moved off down the stream.

The boy went slowly, and Merlin had time to take care of his own necessities before he followed. Woodland streams could be deceptive, but eventually they all flowed downhill. Artor had correctly judged that this tributary would in time reach the Wae, where he could find the road that would take him southward again and home. It was only a matter of keeping his nerve and keeping on.

Will he thank me for the adventure? wondered the druid, *or will he be angry with me for abandoning him?*

Perhaps it was a little of both, for as the journey continued, Artor's set features relaxed, and he paused more often to watch the glittering dance of the dragonflies over the water, or the swift dart of a swallow above the trees. Once he surprised a lordly stag who had come down to drink, and they stared at each other in mutual astonishment that turned on the boy's part to awe before the deer, deciding this two-legged creature posed no threat to him, stalked away.

This is my gift to you, thought Merlin, watching. *Whatever you may inherit from your father, this is your inheritance from me.*

And so they continued on as the sun rose past her nooning and began to arch westward. The trees were still too thick to see the end of the forest, but Merlin knew that the road was near. He lagged behind to put on his crumpled garments, intending to double around to meet the boy on the road. And so, Artor was out of sight when the wind shifted and Merlin smelled the rank scent of a bear.

For an instant, shock held him immobile. He had encountered bears in the northern hills and avoided them, for their tempers were uncertain, and nothing less than a band of armed men could make them afraid. He had not thought any still roamed in these hills.

Then, skirts flapping, he began to run. Self-castigation could come later, when he had saved the boy, or failed. Even in the tunic he went swiftly, but before the boy was in sight he heard the bear's cough of warning. Moving silently, lest his presence set off the attack he feared, he covered the last few feet to the stream.

The bilberries were thick here, growing nearly to the water, and Artor had stopped to pick them, apparently surprising a bear who had come this way with the same thing in mind. It was still standing half-reared in the midst of the bushes, trying to decide whether this two-legged being was a threat.

It was a young bear, perhaps a season separated from its mother, big enough to be dangerous, but perhaps not old enough to have learned to hate humankind. Artor stood absolutely still, the bilberries he had already picked still cupped in his hand. All the color had left his face, but his eyes were very bright. He looked, thought Merlin, *present*, as if by danger the essence of his being had been focused and revealed. At that moment he saw in Artor a spirit that burned like a flame, and knew that men would follow him.

If he lived.

The bear's wet black nose wrinkled as it sniffed the unfamiliar scent mingled with that of the fruit. Branches crackled as it moved toward Artor. The druid drew breath to cry out, but the boy was stretching out his hand, fingers folded flat as if he were offering grain to a pony. The bear lowered its heavy head, and a rough pink tongue swept the berries from Artor's palm. Its sun-bleached brown fur was exactly the color of the boy's hair.

The bear nosed at his hand, then licked his berry-stained cheek, and Artor lifted his other hand and gently stroked the thick fur. For a few moments they stood, man-cub and bear-cub together, then the bear snorted, dropped to all fours, and moved off through the bushes.

The blood pounded in Merlin's head as he remembered to breathe. Artor blinked a few times, then he turned, eyes widening only a little as if after what had just happened the appearance of the druid was no surprise.

"Did you see?" he whispered.

"I saw—" Years of discipline gave Merlin his voice again. "You are Arktos, the Bear, and your totem has blessed you."

IX

THE BIRDS OF BATTLE

A.D. 473

"THE COMMAND WILL HAVE TO GO TO LEUDONUS—" THE KING'S words came out like a curse. "If he can stop ploughing your daughter's field long enough to get into his armor!"

The warm light of a summer's morning on the Tamesis reflected through the window of the old Roman tower and glimmered on the whitewashed ceiling; a clear, pitless light that illuminated his face and showed every line worn there by the past year's pain.

"Uthir!" Igierne shook her head, torn between anxiety and exasperation. He must be feeling particularly bad today, for in general when she was present he guarded his tongue. "Morgause is pregnant with their second child, and Gualchmai is just a year old."

"Two brats in three years is a good yield," growled the king. "Time we made sure there's something for them to inherit. Leudonus is the best of the lot—if I can't take the field he'll have to command."

"That is why you gave him Morgause in marriage," Igierne reminded him.

"Hoped it wouldn't come to this— Damn!" He swore again as he tried to shift position on the bed. It was as comfortable as his household could make it, but the old garrison fort had

143

never been intended for long habitation. Londinium was a commercial city, not a fortress, and the old tower, with the river to the south and a rampart and ditch between it and the city, was the safest place they could find.

In the past three years the episodes of joint pain and muscular weakness had become ever more frequent. At times, when the weather was mild, Uthir would be free of it, but Octha and his warband would not wait on the king's convenience. Hengest's son had kept the oath he swore when he escaped from Londinium, and the army he had raised among the tribes of Germania had made a landfall in the country south of Eburacum.

"My lord, be easy," said Jordanus. "I will send the message by swift riders. If the enemy strikes north, he will be ready."

"And if they move south?" asked Igierne.

Uthir frowned. "Cataur of Dumnonia is energetic, and so are his brothers, but he doesn't have the experience. Catraut is a good fighter, but headstrong. Maybe Eldaul . . . but some still don't trust him. We've worn out our best men in these endless wars! If they come south . . . I'll have to get myself out of this damned bed . . . somehow." He tried to raise himself and fell back again, grunting with pain.

Igierne knelt by his side, wiping the sudden perspiration from his brow. She kept a smile on her lips, but she was weeping within. All his life Uthir had been a warrior—he could have faced death in battle gladly, but not this invisible enemy that was making him a prisoner in his own body. There must be something that would ease this lingering agony!

That night she dreamed of blood and battle, but just as the darkness was about to engulf both friend and foe, light flamed in the west, and she saw riding through the carnage a figure with Uthir's brown hair, grasping in his hand a blazing sword. Where its radiance fell, the Saxons hid their eyes and fled, but the British rose up like souls on the Day of Judgment, crying out in praise of the High King.

"The Sword of Kings. . . ."

She woke in the dawning, whispering its name. Her dream

fled away, but the image of that burning blade remained before her. She sat up, drawing the covers around her against the morning chill.

Decision came to her. "I will bring the Sword from the Isle of Maidens. Its power will make the High King whole!"

The House of the Sword had that indefinable air of damp and emptiness that marks a place not often used. Or perhaps not quite empty—Igierne's gaze moved to the shrouded shape in the center of the chamber. Even covered, she could sense the presence of the Hallow it concealed, but the energies of the Chalybe blade were muted, as if it dreamed. Brows bent in concentration, she returned to her sweeping. It had always been her task to clean this chamber when she lived on the Isle. But today would be different. Today, she would unsheath the Sword.

Ebrdila had sought to dissuade her, but she could not stand against the queen's resolve. Morgause might well have argued, for she had never had any great love for Uthir, but Morgause was Leudonus's broodmare now.

Igierne had made her preparations carefully. The old sheath had fallen to dust years ago, but she had prepared a box, bound in iron and lined with crimson silk, to carry the Sword. For a week she had taken no fleshmeat, and today, only water. She could not rival Merlin in knowledge of the stars, but she knew enough to calculate an auspicious configuration, and to perform this rite at the waxing of the moon.

When she had cleansed the chamber, she went back to the lake for her own purification, shivering as the chill water touched her skin. Only the lapping of the little wavelets against the shore disturbed the hush that lay upon the lake. It had often seemed to her that the great hills gave off silence as the sun gives off light. Here, it was very easy to listen to the voice of the soul. Perhaps that was why the priestesses had made it their sanctuary.

She sat back on her heels, letting the cool morning air dry her skin. *I may be a grandmother, but I am still young and strong.*

And the Sword will restore my beloved! That was the voice of her will, she knew it. But if her soul had any different wisdom, even in this silence she could not hear.

As the sun was nearing the heights of noon, Igierne put on her crimson robe and entered the House of the Sword. Twelve dark-clad priestesses stood in a circle around her, chanting softly, drawing power from the earth as she drew strength from them.

"Cocidius, Belutacadros, Mars of the Soldiers—" she whispered.

"Hear and bless us . . ." chorused the priestesses.

"Star of Hope, Hand of Justice, Pillar of Power—" And indeed, Igierne could feel the power increasing; she scarcely heard the other women now.

"Sword of the Defender, Sword of Kings, Sword of God!"

She twisted the red cock's neck and the blood flowed over the stone, and then, as in the world outside the sun reached her zenith, grasped the swordhilt, twisted, and pulled the Sword out of the stone.

"For Britannia I draw this blade, and for her lawful king!" With trembling arms she held the weapon high, and the shining steel refracted the light of the torches in red lightnings around the room.

The priestesses recoiled, but Igierne stiffened, shuddering as she tried to control the uprush of power. Behind her closed eyelids cities burned; she saw a crimson sky, swinging swords and bloody spears. In another instant the bloodlust of the blade would overcome her—

—and in that moment of panic the spirit of the sword-priest who was her ancestor spoke within her and she remembered the words that she must say.

"Fortitude binds fury. . . . Strength binds savagery. . . . Right binds rapine. . . . Lord of the Sword I summon Thee; control Thy power!"

For a breath longer the blade's hunger blazed; then something immense and ancient and cold descended from on high to enclose it, and Igierne was left gasping, hanging onto the sword. With her last strength she dragged it into the box, for it had grown heavy with the power it contained. She closed the lid, and then her knees gave way and she sat down beside it on the cold floor.

Igierne had waited almost too long. While she was traveling to the Isle of Maidens and claiming the Sword, Leudonus and his army were halting Octha's northern campaign. Just after Beltain they fought a great battle near Eburacum, and though it ended in victory for the British, Leudonus's forces had been too well savaged to pursue their advantage, and the Saxons retreated unhindered toward Londinium.

Now, the great city's inadequate defenses turned to its advantage, for the enemy wanted a walled town where they could halt and lick their wounds in safety. Just north of Londinium lay Verulamium, and there Octha took refuge.

As Igierne came back down the Roman road, she encountered roving scouts who told her that the army of Southern Britannia was beseiging Verulamium, where the martyr Albanus had his shrine, and that the Pendragon had had himself carried there in a litter so that he could command.

"You should have stayed on the Isle," said Uthir when he saw her. "You'd have been safe there."

"My mother may have been Lady of the Lake, but my father was a warrior who died on the Night of the Long Knives. I hope my courage is no less than his."

Uthir cleared his throat gruffly, but his eyes had kindled when he saw her, and she knew he was glad to have her at his side. Indeed, the excitement seemed to have distracted him from his troubles, and though he looked feverish, he did not seem to be in so much pain as before.

They had found quarters for the king in a partly ruined villa near the town. That evening, the British commanders gathered in what had been the dining chamber for a council of war.

"Another few days of siege and we'll have them!" exclaimed Cataur.

Still young enough to be enthusiastic, there were times when he reminded Igierne painfully of his uncle Gorlosius, but he seemed to bear the High King no enmity for a death which had, after all, put him in line to inherit Dumnonia. His wife had recently borne him a son whom they named Constantine, for they were descended from the grandfather of Uthir in the female line.

"But do we want them—" objected Eldaul, "if it means a house-to-house fight where we can make no use of our cavalry?"

"Do you propose to leave them there unmolested?" Cataur replied.

"Of course not," said Ulfinus. "Give them a good scare on the walls, and perhaps we can winkle them out of there!"

Matauc of Durnovaria, who had created a princedom from the old Durotrige lands, shook his head. "Beseige them long enough and they'll starve to death inside!" Leonorus of the Belgae, who was even more cautious by nature, nodded agreement.

"We don't have that long," exclaimed Ulfinus. "It is high summer now—if there is to be a harvest, our men must be getting away home!"

"There is a way." Merlin, who as usual had been effectively invisible until he wished to be heard, came forward. Several of the commanders jumped, and one of them crossed himself.

"The Saxons are concerned above all with their reputation as warriors. They will pursue glory even to their own disadvantage. You complain, my lord, that your weakness will not allow you to fight—" He turned to Uthir. "Let it work for you. Have them carry you in your litter before the walls, and let your men mock the enemy by saying they are too cowardly to fight even a man who cannot ride."

Uthir flushed angrily. "And what about my honor?"

"Is it dishonor to tell the truth?" Merlin spoke dispassionately, but Igierne could see the sorrow in his eyes.

"It's not, but you're the only man who would dare say it to me—" growled the king.

"And what if it works, and they come out to fight us?"

Jordanus said into the silence that followed. "We can use our cavalry then, but they still have the greater numbers. We must not only win, but win so decisively that the Saxons will run away to lick their wounds and not come back again!"

"Merlin . . ." the king said slowly. "In all these years I've never required you to take a role in the fighting. But I'm asking now, for I see no other way. Can't you find a spell to cast madness on the enemy? To call spirits from the earth to fight them?"

Those parts of the druid's face not covered by beard went perfectly white. Igierne realized suddenly how much silver there was in her cousin's hair.

"You don't know . . . the cost of what you're suggesting—"

"Maybe not. But I think you know what it costs me to ask!"

For a long moment dark eyes met gray, and it was the druid who first looked away.

"I do . . ." whispered Merlin. "I will do what I may."

From there, the conversation turned to ways of disposing of their forces if the plan to draw the enemy out should succeed. Merlin went out almost immediately, and presently the others also took their leave and went away.

"They're so hot for the fight," Uthir said painfully. "I'd give my soul to stand with them, but I can hardly hold a sword!"

"There is a Sword that I think you could hold," Igierne said softly, "and it will not require your soul, but only your promise to serve this land."

"I gave that at my anointing—" he began, not understanding.

Igierne shook her head, pulling the long box from beneath the cloak she had laid over it and laying it on the bed beside him. "This belongs to an older mystery." Feeling her own heart beat faster, she opened the box and turned back the cloths that wrapped the Sword.

"Touch it—"

Uthir gripped the hilt and jerked, let go, then carefully grasped it once more. The color came and went in his face as power pulsed through him, then, with an effort of will, he released the hilt and covered it with the silk again.

"By Beli's blazing balls!" he breathed, which if not precisely the same god, at least belonged to the right religion. "That thing will either kill or cure me! Where—"

"It will cure you!" Igierne exclaimed. "It must!" She could not allow herself to contemplate any other possibility, for he had pulled the box closer to his body, and it was clear that he would never now give up the Sword.

And so, as the British prepared for battle around them, Igierne recounted to her king the history of the Chalybe blade.

Merlin watched, frowning, as Uthir's litter was carried onto the battlefield. Behind him, the British were moving into position before the western gate of Verulamium. Smaller forces had been delegated to watch the other gateways, but it was here, where broad pastures spread out to either side of the road, that the major fighting must be. Overhead the sky was clear, but to the west, gray clouds were building, and a restless wind bent the grass.

The men seemed grim, but determined; there had been little rest for anyone the night before, as warriors sharpened weapons and checked the straps of their armor or simply sat by their campfires, too tense to sleep.

Merlin's preparations had been more complex, if less tangible, as he searched his memory for the appropriate spells and contemplated the ways in which they must be focused and combined. He calculated their interaction as carefully as a master chef making choices from his spice jars. But a cook could only ruin a meal; if Merlin made a mistake, both armies might be destroyed. When he tried to rest, his sleep was troubled by images of destruction from whose midst rose a flaming sword.

Uthir had given them their instructions with a kind of febrile gaiety that Merlin found disturbing. Was he fey, or had the prospect of battle simply made him forget his pain? Either way, he should not be out there. Merlin had only meant to suggest that Uthir have himself carried before the walls to taunt the

Saxons, not station himself in the midst of the battle line. Even if the British did not win this battle, their cause would not be lost while the High King lived. He had to survive long enough for Artor to grow up.

Thus the druid in him had reasoned, but as he watched the king go by, the tears on his cheeks were those of the man.

He turned his attention inward, seeking solace from that invisible companion who had been his inspiration and comfort for so long.

"I give life—I do not take it. I cannot help you here. What you do today will be done on your own. . . ."

"So be it—" whispered Merlin, but there was a knot of unease in his belly that would not go away.

"Hai, you Saxon dogs!" cried the British warriors, "why are you hiding behind those walls? Are you afraid to face us? Even our sick are a match for you! Come out and play!"

From beyond the wall they heard shouting, then above the gate a Saxon head appeared.

"We have no need for children's games," came the guttural answer. "We are men!"

Another helmed head appeared beside him. "What honor is there in killing a man who is half-dead already? Take your king home and let him die in peace!"

Merlin looked up and saw a buzzard circling hopefully. He climbed into one of the wagons where no one would trip over him, lay down, and sent his awareness arrowing upward to seize the mind of the bird, then directed it to fly toward the town.

"Skulk inside there and starve if you want to," called the British, "but we give you a chance to settle this now. The only peace between us will be in the grave. See, we will withdraw to give you room!"

The escort surrounding Uthir's litter began to retreat. The buzzard soared over the walls. Through the bird's eyes, Merlin could see Saxon warriors crowding toward the walls, knots of men tangling and separating as they argued.

"Pee-oo," called the buzzard, *"Fight, kill, win—"* Carried by

the force of his will, the message arrowed down. *"Charge, strike, destroy! Pee-oo, pee-oo, pee-oo. . . ."*

This time the noise from inside the town was louder. The fair-haired man who had first replied seemed to be arguing with the others. It was Octha, Hengest's son. Merlin guided the buzzard closer.

"Pee-oo, pee-oo, blood will flow and I will feast! Go out and win glory!" Three times widdershins he circled the Saxon leader, then winged out past the gateway, and Octha's disputation became a battle cry.

The gate trembled as men hurried to draw the bar, then swung open. The Saxon warriors began to form up into their battle array.

Soaring back towards the British, Merlin saw their spearmen ready, the cavalry wings waiting to either side. Uthir's litter was still in the center, but the High King was sitting up now, speaking to his men.

"The Saxons called me the half-dead king," Uthir burst out laughing, "because I lay flat in my litter, felled by illness. And it was true, but I'd rather fight them half-dead than live healthy as a horse and have them think me afraid! Better to die with honor than live disgraced!"

From the gateway came the thunder of spear-shafts beating on shields.

"Do you hear them, lads? They are coming out—will you show them how rough the men of Britannia can play?"

The British replied with an ululation of defiance whose echoes left a mist of brightness in the air. Merlin released the buzzard and sank back into his body. Even with his eyes closed, he could sense the High King's presence as a radiant sphere of power. Had the exultation of the moment released some potential the druid had never noticed before, as Artor had been transfigured by meeting the bear? Or was it something else—

There was no time to wonder. Octha and his warriors were coming out of Verulamium. More and more of them poured through the gate. The mournful call of a cowhorn sounded above the noise and the drumming of spear on shield gave way to the thunder of feet on sod as they began to run.

From the British side trumpets blared. The sound of thunder was abruptly amplified as from one side, Cataur of Dumnonia and his horsemen, and from the other, Eldaul and his cavalry, began their own charge. The wood of the wagon shivered to the vibration. Merlin got to his feet, holding to the side for balance, just as the charge hit, and the separate groups of combatants became a single struggling mass.

In moments, Uthir was surrounded, as in the game of *tabula* the enemy pieces attack the warriors guarding the king. The clangor of clashing weapons smote the ear, pierced by the cries of those who were struck down. Merlin had been present at other battles, but before, he had always waited with the physicians. Now he forced himself to really look at the carnage, striving to understand what was happening.

The Saxons were experienced fighters. Once the British had charged, they lost their main advantage. Horsemen skirmished around the edge of the battle, picking off foes with their lances, but they could not affect the fighting farther in. The British were going on the defensive. This, then, was why Uthir had insisted that the druid help them; without Merlin's magic to tip the balance, the British might well lose.

Once more he sat down. This time, he could not merely ride a passing raptor; he must *become* it. Focusing inward, he formed the image of the raven, Cathubodva's bird.

Goddess, it is your people who are suffering—come to us, blast our foes!

His breathing grew deeper; awareness of his body faded, to be replaced by an alien sense of taut strength, of lightness, of the air. Spirit borne by the raven, he opened his eyes, spread wings to catch the wind, and beat heavily into the sky.

To spirit sight, the forms of the men locked in that mortal struggle were no more than shadows. What he saw was their spirit bodies, flaring brightly as courage spurred them against the foe or fading as they were overcome. Those whose lives were severed floated free, gazing down in confusion at the battle in which they could no longer join.

The raven dove downward, beak opening in the terrible cry with which the Lady of Battles freezes the courage of her foes. Glossy feathers flared white in the light of the sun. And though fleshly ears might hear nothing, the souls of the Saxons heard, and quailed. That moment of hesitation put heart into the British warriors, who drove with renewed vigor at their enemies.

The raven, flapping skyward once more, saw a knot of combatants at whose center swayed Octha's fair head. They were perilously close to the High King; Octha could reach him in a moment if he broke free. The raven circled, gathering momentum, but before he could dive, two dark shapes sped between her and her goal—two other ravens, cawing defiance, which Merlin heard as words.

"This man is my kin through many sons . . . I remember!" called the first raven, and Merlin recalled that Hengest's family believed themselves to be descended from one of their gods.

"I protect him, for he plans wisely and well—" the other echoed.

"What is that to me?" Cathubodva's voice came through her bird. *"He has attacked my land and killed my people! He must die!"*

There were two of the enemy ravens, but the one who was Cathubodva was bigger. Wheeling and slashing, they joined in a battle as furious as the one below, the German god and the Celtic goddess confronting one another.

Even the overflow of power from that conflict of forces was enough to madden the human warriors. Shrieking and grunting, they dropped their weapons and went for each other with teeth and fingernails. The impact of that violence reverberated from one plane of existence to the next. Merlin felt his own mind disintegrating into a madness in which he had no thought but to rend and slay.

And then the fabric of the world was rent by a Sword of Light, and a great Voice that cried out—

"Stop! If they must fight, they shall do so within the bounds I establish—not as beasts, but as men!"

From the Sword came the shape of a Warrior. To some He

seemed the helmed Mars of the old shrines, and to some, red Cocidius of the Wall. To the Saxons, He appeared grim and tall, with only one hand. He lifted the blazing sword and swept it above the battlefield, and everywhere combatants sprang apart, staring about them like men waking from a dream.

But the power of that stroke swept Merlin back to his own body, and for some little while he knew no more.

Merlin opened his eyes and groaned. His head hurt—indeed, every part of his body ached as badly as if he had been out on the battlefield. In a sense, he thought painfully, it was true. He should have anticipated that his astral activities would be reflected in his physical body. He sat up, wincing. Then he remembered.

Fear sent its own anodyne through his body as he jumped down from the wagon, but now there was nothing to distract him from the images that flooded his memory. And there before him was the reality of the battlefield. Where there had been green fields was now a trampled mass of mud and blood and the remains of men. Already the ravens—the real ones—were gathering. With all his senses still open, he felt the agony of the wounded, the confused spirits of the slain.

My fault . . . he thought. *It was I who made this a conflict of forces beyond the nature of humankind.*

In the distance he could see fleeing figures; a few horsemen were chasing them. The British were not running. From that, he supposed that they must have won. He certainly could not tell from looking at men's faces. They all looked as stunned as he. But they did not carry his guilt. Already he could feel the madness that had driven him to the mountains once before nibbling at his control. Rubbing his forehead, he looked around him. Where was the king?

In the center of the carnage, men were moving. They lifted the litter and bore it slowly toward the villa, stopping often to rest, for all had wounds of their own. Leaning on his staff, Merlin hurried to meet them.

Uthir opened his eyes as the druid bent over him. He was splashed with blood, but none of it seemed to be his own.

"Octha's dead—" he whispered. "We have the field."

Merlin nodded. "My lord, how is it with you?"

"As if I've been ploughed . . . by a red-hot poker." Uthir coughed painfully, and lifted his mantle so that Merlin could see what he had hidden there.

The druid stopped short, appalled recognition making everything suddenly very clear. He had never seen the full length of the Chalybe sword until now, when it gleamed with deadly beauty at the king's side. Now he understood where Igierne had gone, and why she had avoided him when she returned.

"I should have known!" Merlin exclaimed. "I sensed its presence—" It was one more thing in which he had failed.

"I didn't have the strength to wield it. The power . . . burned through me . . . killed everyone around."

"And no matter what Igierne may have said, you did not have the right," the druid replied.

Uthir grimaced. "Don't tell her . . . she'll blame herself. Must . . . keep it safe. . . ."

"I also am of the blood of its keepers. I will guard the Sword for your son, who is its destined lord." He pulled off his cloak, and kneeling beside the litter, wrapped it around the blade.

"I'm sorry I won't see him grown. . . . I always thought there would be time. Give him a father's blessing for me. . . ."

Merlin looked down at that white face and nodded.

The king smiled faintly. "But at least . . . Octha is dead."

Some of the servants who had stayed with Igierne at the villa came out, saw the litter, and began to run toward them. Merlin stepped back, still watching Uthir, as they took him up and carried him inside.

For a few moments Merlin stood unmoving, the shrouded Sword held close against his breast. Overhead, ravens were flying, calling harshly to their kin. Already he could smell a charnel scent from the battlefield. If he stayed here, with the Sword, he would indeed go mad. He took a deep breath, drawing up a cloak of shadow around him. Then he strode swiftly away.

Merlin had planned, insofar as thinking was possible, to carry the weapon northward, back to the Isle. But three days later, when the daze in which he had been wandering began to lift at last, he found himself many miles to the southwest. The Saxons had raided through this land several times, and many of the villas and farmsteads were in ruins, but there were buildings enough left to shelter him, and food in the gardens that had been left to run wild.

Only Calleva, on the old Roman road, still maintained itself as a center of civilization. Near an abandoned chapel just outside of the town Merlin came to rest.

"*Stop here . . .*" said his daimon.

"*Make me a house,*" said the god in the Sword.

When Merlin began to rebuild the roof, folk from the town decided he must be a hermit, and some of them started to leave food as an offering. They were not so far wrong, though his devotions were not quite what they might have expected. As the days passed, he fell into a trance of labor in which the task of rebuilding kept his madness away.

He repaired the roof, and thatched it securely. He brought stones and mud with which to repair the shattered wall. While he was gathering them he had noted a boulder half his height, and almost as wide. When all else was done he went out during the night, and chanting to focus his strength, managed to roll it inside. Then, using a chisel and mallet that he had found in an outbuilding, he began to carve into the stone a new channel in which to sheathe the Sword.

It was precise and patient work. Long before he completed it he heard men in the road outside the chapel, talking of the death of the High King. Some whispered of poison, but others said it was only that he had exhausted his last strength in the battle. It was said that his queen was bringing the body to the Giant's Dance to lie with that of his brother and the British lords.

Merlin remembered a Samhain Eve beside the sacred stones and the wonder in Uthir's eyes, and wept, but he did not stop chiseling at the stone.

There were more rumors after that, as first one lord and then another sought support in order to claim the overlordship of Britannia. But there was no one on whom all the princes could agree.

The autumn was well advanced by the time Merlin finished his work at last, and slid the Sword into the channel with the secret twist that prevented anyone who did not know the secret from drawing it out again. And when it was sheathed, he carved into the front of the stone these words—

Quicunque me distringet rex iustus Britanniae est . . .

Then, at last, the compulsion released him. Over Sword and stone he draped his mantle, and walked out of the little chapel for the last time.

A ghost of the man he had been whispered that he should go to Igierne in Londinium, or to Artor in Demetia. But he no longer trusted his own wisdom. Let the men who lusted to rule Britannia and the gods they served do the fighting. He had had enough of humankind.

Merlin's feet carried him northward, traveling by night and speaking to no one. By the time he reached the Wall it was hard to remember human language, and so he passed into the shadows of the Forest of Caledonia and disappeared from the knowledge of men.

THE SWORD IN THE STONE

A.D. 475

IN HER DREAM, IGIERNE WAS SITTING IN AN APPLE TREE.

Cradled in its branches and rocked by the wind, she watched the slow-wheeling stars, yet even as she marveled at their majesty she knew that these visions were not hers but those of another, whose dream she shared.

Her tree was surrounded by oak and ash and stately pines, for the forest had grown over an old orchard and only the single apple tree remained. Hungry, she reached for an apple; the arm that moved was long, sinewy, and covered with coarse hair. Abruptly she realized whose mind she shared.

"Merlin," she called, "where are you? We feared you dead— Britannia needs you, I need you!"

"I am the Wild Man of Caledonia. . . . Merlin is a dream. Are you my little lass? I have seen you in a moonbeam, Lady, but you do not speak to me anymore. . . ." Through his eyes she saw leaves that glittered in the moonlight and the pale shapes of distant hills.

"It is Igierne who calls you. Return from your wanderings!"

He bit into the apple, and she felt the swift rush of sweetness on her own tongue.

"Merlin loved Igierne, when he was a man. . . . The Wild Man loves the little pig that roots beneath his tree. . . ."

For a moment surprise and pity held her silent, then need

drove her on. *"If you ever loved me, find my son! The princes tear at this poor land like ravens at a carcass, and only he can make it whole—"*

A sudden wave of anguish blurred her vision; she smelled once more the deathly reek of the battlefield. Then the image faded, but the sorrow remained.

"Let the White Raven beware the Raven of Battle. To Calleva come the princes in search of sovereignty. . . . Where you find the Sword you shall find the King. . . ."

Branches tossed as he climbed downward. The ground blurred beneath her vision as he began to run, faster and faster until his awareness dissolved into pure motion and Igierne's consciousness fell away.

She opened her eyes, grasping for memories that were already fast fading, but on her lips the taste of apple remained.

How long had it been, she wondered, since she had awakened with happiness in her heart? Whatever her dream meant, it was better than nightmares in which Uthir died in her arms yet again. She had buried him in the barrow by the Giant's Ring, as he had asked, and then begun the long journey back to the north, staying for a time in one town and then in another, until she came to Isca in Demetia, where Bishop Dubricius had welcomed her.

Igierne was in no hurry to continue on, for what remained for her, even at the Lake, but to live out an empty existence mourning the death of Britannia's joy and her own?

But today she had hope once more, hope, and a fragment of prophecy. Bishop Dubricius was accounted a wise man. Together, perhaps they could make one last attempt to persuade the warring princes to seek unity.

In Calleva, one could almost believe that Rome had never departed from the Isle. Its walls were intact, its amphitheater only a little overgrown, its gracious houses, set amidst their gardens and orchards, still the homes of cultured men. It was also convenient in location, far enough to the west to be out of easy reach of Saxon raiders, and connected to the rest of the country by good roads. If summoning the lords of Britannia to this place had been no more than a night fancy, thought Igierne, then it had been a useful one.

For the warlords and chieftains and magistrates were coming in.

During the two years since Uthir's death there had been no central authority. Hengest, recovering from the shock of Octha's loss, had designated his grandson Oesc as heir, and though he no longer took the field, the chieftains he had summoned from Germania were swift to fall upon their British neighbors. In the North, Colgrin and Baldulf had made alliance with the old enemy, the Picts and Scots, and were extending their holdings. In the West the lords of Demetia and Guenet fought the men of Eriu and each other.

But now, when the first winter storms were putting an end to the fighting season, the British had braved bad roads and wild weather to converge on the old *civitas* of the Atrebates. The chieftains and their families were given hospitality in the better homes of the town, while the lesser lords and *gentiles* set up camp, with their men, in the fields outside. Even Leudonus had left the Votadini lands in charge of his clan chiefs and come south to the conclave, and with him came Morgause.

Igierne was sitting in the atrium of the chief magistrate, made pleasant by shrubs in pots and beds of late-blooming flowers, when a light step on the flagstones made her turn and she saw that her daughter had arrived.

Though the atrium was protected from the wind, Morgause's draperies fluttered with supressed motion. Clearly, marriage and motherhood agreed with her. What the girl's face had lost in childish roundness, her breasts had gained, and her complexion was blooming. Igierne frowned in sudden suspicion.

"Morgause, are you breeding again?"

Quick color came and went in the girl's face, then she set her hands over her belly and smiled.

"I shall have three children in four years of marriage. In all your years as a wife, you never managed but the two!"

Igierne's eyes widened a little at the taunt; she had not meant to sound disapproving—well, not very.

"I congratulate you on being one of those women who are built for bearing." She managed an answering smile. "Your husband must be pleased."

"I will give him enough sons to defend the North with the fruit of my own womb! Or perhaps they will rule a greater kingdom. Clearly, Uthir meant Leudonus to be his heir."

"Certainly he respected Leudonus's abilities as a commander," Igierne said evenly. "But the lords of southern Britannia may feel that his strength lies too far away."

Morgause shrugged and paced across the stones. Her mantle was dyed a deep crimson, not the color that had clashed so with her complexion at her wedding, but a shade like Gaulish wine. Heavy earrings of gold and garnet hung in her ears, and her golden pennanular brooch was set with garnets as well. Igierne remembered when she used to adorn herself in jewels. She had worn only black since Uthir died.

With a swirl of her skirts Morgause turned to face her once more.

"That argument might be used against any of them. At least Leudonus *has* strength. I will be Tigernissa, and it will be your turn, mother, to sit on the Isle of Maidens and watch the world go by!"

"Oh, the Lady of the Lake can do a little more than that—" said Igierne tightly. "Did you learn nothing when you were there?"

"I learned a great deal. And I am learning more in the North, where they revere their queens. Leudonus's mother was a princess of the Picts, who trace their descent through the female line. They choose their husbands to defend the land, but they are the source of power."

Igierne picked up her embroidery again and took a stitch or two. What Morgause had said agreed with the secret teaching of the Isle, but southern Britannia had been Roman too long, and the men who ruled it had forgotten many things.

"Neither queen nor king is the source of sovereignty," she said at last, "but the Goddess Herself who is Lady of this land. Do not forget that, daughter. Whatever I have done or you shall do, we are only Her deputies."

Morgause responded with a rather odd smile. "Oh, I have not forgotten. But the Lady sometimes wears a different face in the northern lands. . . ."

Igierne raised one eyebrow, but before she could inquire she heard voices in the entry and another woman, draped in a gown and palla of dusty blue, came into the atrium, followed by a lanky boy.

"*Domina*—" She made a reverence to Igierne, and then, after a moment's hesitation, to Morgause. "I do not know if you will remember me, for it has been many years—"

"Of course I do! You are Flavia, wife of Caius Turpilius." And indeed, though Flavia's figure had become more matronly, she had not really changed. "I am glad that you and your husband have come. They will need his good sense at the Council."

Flavia nodded. "He and young Cai are down at the meadow where the warriors will show off their strength in the games. God send that it does not become a battlefield!"

"Will not your younger son be fighting?"

For a moment Flavia looked troubled, then she smiled. "He is only fifteen, though he is taller than Cai. Time enough for him to be fighting when he has grown into his bones. . . ." She looked fondly at the boy, who flushed red as he realized he was the center of attention.

He reminded Igierne of a young colt, still all legs and neck, but with the promise of grace and speed. At least his skin was not disfigured by the spots that afflicted so many lads that age.

"If he has the time, perhaps you would lend him to me as an escort," she said to Flavia. "I no longer have a real household, and the town has become very crowded as the chieftains come in."

"Too crowded . . ." Morgause said softly, eyeing the new-comers.

Igierne frowned at her. Why should Morgause care if her mother showed some kindness to this gangling boy? But clearly it was so. *She still wants my approval*, thought the queen, *despite all her proud words.*

"I would be honored—" The boy spoke for the first time. If he resented being shuffled off among the ladies he was too well-bred to let it show.

"Come to me tomorrow," said Igierne. "You may be my escort to the warriors' games."

"My children in Christ, to this place I have called you to take counsel for the safety of your own children and the future of this land."

Bishop Dubricius stood on the dais at the end of the basilica, illuminated by light from the upper windows, which picked out the golden embroidery on his robes. He was a humble man, who on ordinary days dressed as simply as any of his monks. But he was not an unworldly one, reflected Igierne, watching from the gallery, and he knew the power of a judicious display of gold.

"The heathen encompass us on every side, and we have been abandoned by the eagles of Rome. Under the authority of our own emperors we have fought them; at times we nearly drove them from our shores. But only when we were united. When each lord cares only for his own lands, the devil's spawn can gobble us piecemeal, like a herd that has been scattered by the wolves!"

From his audience came a murmur of appreciation, if not for his text, at least for his rhetoric. The farther windows lit them as well, glinting on swordhilts and brooches and torques of gold.

The basilica of Calleva was second only to that of Londinium. The nave was seventy feet high, arches supported the upper walls and separated it from the aisle. In happier times, the decurions of the district had met there to conduct the business of government; now the benches were filled by nearly a hundred proud men from all over the Island.

"Indeed, your grace." Cataur of Dumnonia, representing his father and his grandfather, the prince Gerontius, rose from his bench to answer. His brother, Gerontius the younger, was at his side. "If we did not agree with you we would not have come here. But there is no man remaining of the direct line of Constantine to inherit, and how else shall we choose?"

His question seemed innocent enough, but every man there knew that through the female line Cataur was descended from the British emperor who had challenged Rome. It occurred to Igierne suddenly that Morgause, through her father, carried that blood as well. Had she thought of that? From the intent way in which she was watching, her mother felt it likely, and if so, Leudonus would be considering it as well.

Despite four centuries of Roman emperors, who were as likely to be raised to the purple for their popularity, or their power, their competence, or sometimes by pure chance, as for their heredity, an honored bloodline still carried weight with these descendents of Celtic kings.

If Uthir had allowed Merlin to bring back their son, thought Igierne, there would have been an heir in the male line. Where was he now, her little boy? Did he know of his heritage? Or was he dead, and had Uthir and Merlin resisted her pleas to bring him to her because they feared to tell her so?

It hardly mattered now. Cataur had just proclaimed himself a candidate. Igierne remembered him as energetic but head-strong, requiring a firm hand. Would he have the self-discipline to rule?

"Who is that?" asked Flavia as Eleutherius got to his feet.

"The prince of Eburacum. His father ruled the lands from the Wall to Lindum, but the Anglians are carving out a home-land there now."

Eleutherius cleared his throat. "Any lord we choose must care for the peoples of the North as well as the South; the remnants who hold out in the East, surrounded by Saxons, as well as the safe western lands. The sons of Ambrosius came

back from Armorica to lead us. We do not want a High King
who will flit oversea to Dumnonia if things go badly here."

That was close enough to a challenge to make all eyes turn
to Cataur, for the northern coast of Armorica had been given
its name by Britons who fled there from the lands his father
had ruled. But before he could answer, Catraut, who had established himself in Verulamium after the battle, spoke in favor
of choosing a man with experience on the Saxon frontier. He
was followed by others, as each region proclaimed its impor-
tance, or its needs.

Throughout all this, Leudonus had sat in silence. He had
put on weight since his marriage to Morgause, but he was still
in his prime, broad rather than tall, with thinning reddish hair.
His mantle was woven in wool of many colors, in the traditional royal style. Igierne had seen him in Roman dress, which
he wore well, and knew that this appeal to Celtic memory must
be deliberate.

*He will let them talk themselves out before he makes his move, and
hope that in their desperation they will accept even a northerner, if
he has sufficient power.*

The light through the windows was deepening toward sunset when Bishop Dubricius held up his crozier. Reluctantly, the
men fell silent.

"We will not decide this issue today, but I think that those
who have spoken have set forth the qualities we must seek in
our king—strength, wisdom, a care for all parts of this land, a
right to rule which can be accepted by everyone here. . . ."

"A miracle . . ." whispered someone nearby.

"Christ Himself in His second coming could not win accep-
tance from them all!" another voice answered.

One of the local men got to his feet. "We will never agree
until God Himself gives us a sign! But in the hermit's chapel
just beyond the town there is a sword thrust into a stone which
no man can pull free. The writing on the rock says it belongs
to the king!"

Igierne sank back against the wall as if she had been struck
to the heart by that same blade.

Her dream of Merlin had been true! And this was what had happened to the Sword, and why he had told her to seek Calleva! But why? Only Merlin and she knew the trick of making a slot that would hold the Chalybe blade. Had he meant her to draw it herself and choose her king as a priestess of the Lady of Sovereignty?

"My lady, are you unwell?" asked Flavia, and Igierne realized that her skin had gone clammy and she was perspiring beneath her veil.

She shook her head, though she was trembling with a sudden awareness of great forces building around her. She dared not touch the Sword, she realized then. She had given it to Uthir, and it had killed him. She straightened, striving for calm. She could not interfere, but she would bear witness to what must come.

The combats had already started when Igierne arrived at the amphitheater, accompanied by Flavia's boy. The horse races were scheduled for later in the day. The amphitheater lay to the northeast of the town, where it caught the morning light, but the day had dawned cloudy; now and again a cool breath of mist touched her skin. She had wrapped up warmly, and the people of Calleva had set up a shelter over part of the seating and made it comfortable with rugs and cushions for the benefit of the noble ladies and the older men.

It was the Bishop's idea that a day of martial displays would relax the chieftains as well as enabling them to judge the temper of each other's men. And it was just as well, she thought, that they should have some time to get over last night's embarassment at having tried to draw the Chalybe Sword from the stone—and failed.

Once more she bit back her anger. *Curse you, Merlin, for preparing this test and then disappearing! If you know who is destined to draw the blade, why are you not here to make sure he does so?*

Originally the amphitheater must have seated nearly the entire population of the town. She guessed it was not now much used, for some of the timbers had decayed, but the stands that remained gave a good view of the arena, whose grass had been cropped by the sheep that ordinarily grazed here into a mat of green.

The boy leaned forward as two new combatants strode onto the green, armed as for war, except for the leather bands that wrapped their swords.

"Who are they?"

"One of Cataur's men and a man from Demetia, by the badges," she said. "I don't know their names. Do you want to be a fighter?"

He looked at her in surprise. "Peace is better than war, but nobody will have peace unless some are willing to spend their lives to guard the others. At least it is so in these times."

"Is that what Caius Turpilius told you?"

"It is what I believe."

His gaze returned to the field. The two men saluted the stands, then faced each other, feet braced and weapons raised.

"But don't you dream of winning honor, or hearing people praise your name?"

He colored, and she knew that she had guessed well.

"If I fought for the right things . . ." he said in a low voice, with a quick glance to see if she was laughing at him.

One of the swords slammed against the opposing shield and he looked back to the field to see the exchange of blows. The fighting settled into a pattern of tense pauses and flurried engagement. It was a shock when the Dumnonian's blade slipped past the enemy guard and stopped just touching the Demetian swordsman where the neck and shoulder joined. Igierne admired his control—if the blow had landed with full force it could have broken the man's neck even with a blunted edge. The Cornovians began to cheer and there was a patter of applause from the stands.

"I had a strange dream last night," the boy said as the next pair came out onto the green. "I was standing in a forge, watching a blacksmith at work, except that it was not a man, but a woman, like one of the old goddesses, with hair of flame. She took the fragments she was hammering from the anvil and cast them into a crucible. But they weren't metal, but the limbs of men. And then she turned and spoke to me—"

He fell silent, frowning. Igierne felt her skin pebble. Who was this boy to have a dream of such power?

"Can you remember her words?"

"All that is made will in the end be broken. I gather the shards and try them in the flame. The dross I skim away, but the true metal runs together, all the stronger for its mixing."

"What happened then?" Igierne asked softly.

"The lumps melted and mingled until they were a single glowing mass. The goddess poured the molten metal into a mold, and when it was solid, she laid it on the anvil and began to hammer it. She hammered it into a sword . . . and when she was done," he swallowed, "she asked if I would serve her, and held it out to me. . . ."

Igierne's heart began to bound unevenly in her breast. "Boy, look at me—" She searched his face, striving to find something familiar in the curly brown hair or the blue eyes. But her own eyes blurred so that it was hard to see. "What is your name?"

"Arktos, because once I met a bear—well, really, it's Artor—"

Or Artorius? If this was her son, clearly he had not been told. She must speak with Flavia!

The boy was still staring at her in amazement when she saw a beefy young man with the Turpilius nose running toward them across the grass.

"Artor, Artor!" He pulled up in front of them, sketched a bow to Igierne, and grasped the rail in front of the boy. "I broke my sword practicing at the post! Run back to the camp and get my good blade—quickly!" He danced from one foot to the other. "I'm due to fight in the next round!"

Igierne looked from Cai to Artor, who was already on his feet, apparently accustomed to being ordered around in this way. "My Lady, do you mind? I will not be long—"

She gestured to him to draw nearer, and said softly, "You will return all the quicker if you stop in the old chapel just beyond the eastern gate and take the sword that is there—"

His face brightened, and he vaulted over the railing and darted away.

Well, Merlin, if that is interference then it is your fault for not being here to stop me, she thought defiantly. *If our blood runs true in him, he will draw the Sword!*

"It was kind of Artor to help you," she said to Cai, who was still standing there.

"Oh, well, he has some funny ideas, but he's a good lad all the same."

Not a bad recommendation from an older brother, she told herself, trying to gauge how long it should take the boy to get to the gate and find the chapel. Was he there already? Could he draw the blade, and if he succeeded, she wondered in sudden fear, what would happen then?

It seemed an eternity before she saw his tall figure across the grass, but Cai seemed surprised at how quickly he had made the journey. Artor was walking, not running, and a bundle, swathed in his cloak, was clasped in his arms. He seemed dazed, as one who has looked on too much light.

Igierne felt her heart begin that heavy beat once more.

"What's wrong? Did you run too fast?" Cai was hurrying toward him. "Here, I'll take it—"

For a moment Artor resisted, then he released the bundle, and Cai fumbled for the hilt.

"Ow! It *burned*!"

The blade slid from his hands and Artor bent to catch it before it could hit the ground. Igierne let out a breath she had not known she held, sudden tears blurring her eyes.

"That's not my sword!" Cai took his smarting fingers out of his mouth to cry. Artor looked at Igierne in appeal.

She got to her feet, pitching her voice to carry, though her vision came and went in waves, as if she looked through fire.

"It is not, nor ever shall be. It is the Sword of Kings that Artor holds, the Chalybe blade that the Defender of Britannia shall bear. By blood he is its rightful heir. Before his birth this destiny was written in the stars!"

Her knees gave way and she sat down again, but she had

said enough. From every side, men were gathering. Caius Turpilius came hurrying forward. His face blanched as he saw
Artor holding the Sword.

"Arktos, lad, where did you get that blade?"

"I found it in the chapel beside the gate. Father, did I do
wrong? *She* said—" He broke off, for Caius, seeing the triumph
in Igierne's eyes, had gone down on one knee before him.

"Boy, the druid told me that your birth was good, but I see
now that you come of higher blood than ever I dreamed of!"

"Father, get up! I don't understand!"

"What he means is that you are my son, Artor, by Uthir the
High King," Igierne said in a shaking voice, "the son that we
entrusted to Merlin when you were a babe, that he might find
you a safe fosterage."

"The druid came to us in the summer of the year Uthir made
the lady Igierne his bride," Caius echoed, "with a boy-child a
few weeks old."

The murmur of commentary from the men who had gathered around them became a clamor as word spread. Now the
great lords were coming, Cataur and Leudonus and Eleutherius, with their champions behind them.

"What is this tale?" challenged Leudonus, fixing Igierne
with his pale gaze.

"This boy is Uthir's son, and he has drawn the Sword!"

Leudonus wheeled round to glare at Artor, who still stood
with the Sword clasped against his breast.

"Do you say so? We'll go back to the chapel and if he proves
it, then, woman, you can explain!"

The word spread fast. By the time the procession reached
the hermit's chapel, most of the chieftains and their men and
half the town beside had joined it. Someone had even sent for
Bishop Dubricius, who arrived, red-faced and puffing, just as
they reached the door. With his usual imperturbable good
sense he began to create order out of the confusion, calling on
the chieftains to calm their men, and selecting, with an unerr-

ing grasp of the politics of the gathering, the witnesses, for it was clear that the chapel would hold barely a dozen men.

In the end, besides the Bishop himself, the group included Leudonus and Cataur, the chief magistrate of Calleva, Eleutherius, Catraut and Eldaul, Ulfinus, who had been Uthir's friend, Igierne, Turpilius, and his son Cai.

And Artor, who looked about him like a beast that scents the hunters closing in. But he was still hanging onto the Sword.

"Don't be afraid, lad," said the Bishop. "The truth will prevail, here on this holy ground."

Artor nodded, and Igierne knew it was not the men he feared, but his destiny.

"Will you swear before God and His holy angels that you drew the Sword you are holding from out this stone?"

All could see that the slot in which it had been fixed was empty. Artor nodded again.

"Then I will ask you to thrust the blade back into the rock, and draw it out once more."

Something grim in the set of the boy's jaw reminded Igierne painfully of Uthir as he moved forward. She heard Ulfinus's breath catch, and knew he saw it too. Artor dropped the swathing cloth, and with a swift turn of the wrist, brought the blade up, positioned it over the slot, and with the twisting movement that Igierne's own muscles remembered, thrust it home.

"There is blood on the stone—" said someone, pointing at the dark stain that had run down into the "r" of the *rex* in the rock surface.

"I cut my hand," said Artor, "when I pulled it out before."

"I have heard that such blades must be blooded when they are drawn," said Eldaul reflectively.

For a moment Artor studied the sheathed Sword, his brows bent in a frown, then he turned to the men. "There it is, as it was before. Try if you will. . . ."

"It has burnt me once already!" exclaimed Cai. "I have no desire to touch it again."

"Well I will try," said Catraut, grinning, "though I have no wish to be High King." He went forward, and though the sword did not burn him, neither could he budge it from the stone.

Cataur tried then, and some of the others, to no avail. And all the while Leudonus watched them, pulling at his beard, his gaze going from the Sword to Igierne and back again.

"I think my wife has told me something about this blade. There is a trick to its sheathing, is there not? Are you so tormented by your grief, my lady, that you have told this poor boy the secret and convinced yourself he is your son?"

"Indeed I know that Sword," Igierne said proudly, "for my family guarded it for many years. But I did not bring it here. And as for the boy—my heart began to whisper to me who he must be, and so I told him where to find the blade. But no more—before Our Lady's throne I swear it. I told him no more! It is not the drawing of the blade, but the wielding that is the test, Leudonus. Let Artor pull it out again for you and see if you can bear its power!"

"Do as she says, my son," Bishop Dubricius said softly. "As you did before . . ."

"I knelt down before the altar and asked God's leave," said Artor, "for I was not quite sure it was right to take something from a shrine." As he spoke, he knelt once more, head bowed in prayer. Then he signed himself and went to the stone. "But I did it all faster, because I was hurrying . . ."

He was not hurrying now. Igierne saw him swallow as he faced the Sword, this time knowing what pulling it out might mean.

He set his hand on the hilt, and she saw him stiffen at the first uprush of power. Then he set his feet more firmly and pulled, the muscles in his forearm rippling as he turned the blade, and with a faint hiss it came free. Artor took a step backward and swung it high, and no man could say after whether it was the last light of sunset coming through the open door that lit the Sword or some radiance from within.

Seen by that light, Artor's face was transfigured as well, the boy's unformed features overlaid with the stern majesty of a king. He brought the blade down and drew the keen edge across his forearm next to the other gash. Once more, blood dripped upon the stone.

"It is speaking to me . . ." he murmured. "It only whispered before—" He turned the flat of the blade against his wounds, and when he lifted it, there were two white scars. He straightened then, resting the weapon across his two palms.

"My son," said Igierne, "what does it say?"

"It tells me that the power to defend is the same as the power to destroy. One must balance the other. It says . . . it is a Sword of Justice, that will endure no lie." His blue gaze lifted to Leudonus's face, and the older man could not look away. "Stretch out your hand, my lord, and prove the truth or falsehood of your suspicions on this blade."

Leudonus did not lack courage, but as he neared Artor his steps slowed, as if he walked against a wind. Still, he managed to grip the golden hilt for a full minute before his features contorted in pain and he wrenched his hand away.

"Do not try to take the Sword again. From this hour to his life's ending it will bear no touch but that of the Defender," said a new voice.

They all turned. Merlin stood in the doorway, leaning on his staff. His hair and beard had grown longer, and he was clad only in a kilt of hide, but the Wild Man no longer looked out of his eyes.

"I took him from his mother's breast and gave him to Turpilius to foster. He is Igierne's son."

"But is he Uthir's?" asked Leudonus, recovering. "It was Gorlosius who visited her at Dun Tagell, as I have heard."

"It was Uthir, in Gorlosius's guise," said Merlin. "And Gorlosius himself lay dead already when the king came to her."

"Then it was not adultery," someone whispered. "Look at his face—who else could he be but Uthir's true son?"

"He is very young—" Eldaul began.

"Then you will advise him," snapped Igierne. "Does it matter whether he is my son or he dropped out of the sky? For many generations my family guarded this Sword. Now it has chosen its King."

She turned to Artor. "Will you accept the trust the Sword has laid upon you? Will you swear to defend, not one region, or one tribe, or one faith, but all this Hallowed Isle?"

Artor knelt before her, the Sword fixed upright before him. In his face shone exaltation, and terror, and joy.

"By this holy blade I do so swear . . ."

PEOPLE AND PLACES

A note on pronunciation:

British names are given in fifth-century spelling, which does not yet reflect pronunciation changes. Initial letters should be pronounced as they are in English. Medial letters are as follows.

SPELLED	PRONOUNCED
p	b
t	d
k/c	(soft) g
b	v (approximately)
d	soft "th" (modern Welsh "dd")
g	"yuh"
m	v
initial ue	w

†

PEOPLE IN THE STORY

CAPITALS = major character
* = historical personnage
( ) = dead before story begins
[ ] = name as given in later literature

*Aelle—chief of the South Saxons

*Agricola Longhand—prince of Demetia

AMBROS/MERLIN, son of Maderun and a Wild Man, druid
and wizard

(*Ambrosius the Elder)

*AMBROSIUS AURELIANUS

AMLODIUS, Protector of Brigantia, husband of Artoria
Argantel

*Antonius Donatus, lord of the Novantae

Artoria Argantel, Lady of the Lake, high priestess of the Old
Faith at the Isle of Maidens

ARTORIUS/ARTOR [Arthur], son of Uthir and Igierne

(Artorius Hamicus Sarmaticus, priest of the Sword and Argantel's grandfather)

Baldulf—a Saxon ally of Octha

Belutacadros, ancient British war god

Blaise, priest, confessor to Maderun

(Brannos [Bran the Blessed], a legendary king)

*Cataur [Cador] of Dumnonia, son of Docomaglos

CAI, [Kay], son of Caius Turpilius, Artor's foster-brother &
companion

Caius Turpilius, Artor's foster father

Carmelidus, king of Moridunon, maternal grandfather of
Merlin

*Categirnus, older son of Vitalinus

*Catelius Decianus, lord of the northern Votadini

Cathubodva, ancient British war goddess, analagous to the
Morrigan

*Catraut, prince of Verulamium

Cerituend, Viaun, Creirbiu and Imacdub, Ceridwen, Gwion, Creidwy and Afagddu, from the old legend of Ceridwen's cauldron

Cocidius, an ancient British war god

*Coelius [Coel Hen], lord of Eburacum

*Colgrin—a Saxon ally of Octha

*Constantine, son of Cataur

*Coroticus, lord of Strathclyde

*Dumnuall [Dyfnwal], daughter's son of Germanianus and Ridarchus' brother, lord of the Southern Votadini

Docmaglos, prince of Dumnonia, second son of Gerontius the elder

*DUBRICIUS, bishop of Isca and primate of Britannia

*Ebissa—nephew of Hengest

Ebrdila, a priestess on the Isle of Maidens

Eldaul, lord of Glevum

Eleutherius, lord of Eburacum

Felix, a Christian priest in the service of Vitalinus

Flavia—wife of Caius Turpilius, Artor's foster-mother

Ganeda [Ganiedda], Merlin's half-sister, wife of Ridarchus

*Germanianus, lord of the southern Votadini

Gerontius the Elder, prince of Dumnonia

*Gerontius the younger, son of Docomaglos

*Gillomanus—an Irish raider

Godwulf, a Saxon thyle in the service of Vitalinus

Gorangonus, prince of Cantium

GORLOSIUS, his elder son

(*Hadrian, emperor A.D. 117–138, builder of the Wall)

*HENGEST, a mercenary warrior from Anglia

*Horsa, Hengest's brother

IGIERNE [Igraine], Artor's mother, the daughter of Amlodius and Argantel

Junius Lupercus, commander of the the warriors who guard the Isle

Kurdalagon, legendary smith of the Sarmatians

LEUDONUS [Lot], king of the Votadini

MADERUN, princess of Moridunon, Merlin's mother
Maglicun, a druid in the service of Vitalinus
Maglos Leonorus of Venta Belgarum, king of the Belgae
(*Magnus Maximus [Maxen Wledig]—emperor of Britannia 383–387)
Martinus, a Christian priest and follower of Augustinus of Hippo
Matauc of Dorchester—king of the Durotriges
Matauc Morbrin [Madoc Morvrinus], Merlin's stepfather
Maugantius, a philosopher in Vitalinus's service
MORGAUSE, daughter of Igierne and Gorlosius, married to Leudonus
*Octha, son of Hengest
*Oesc, son of Octha and Hengest's heir
Pascentius—a Frisian raider
Peretur [Peredur], son of Eleutherius, lord of Eboracum
Reginwynna [Rowenna], daughter of Hengest, wife of Vitalinus
*Ridarchus [Rhydderch], king at Altacluta
(Rigantona, daughter of Gutuator, Argantel's grandmother)
*Johannes Riothamus—a British warlord in Gallia
Sulpicius—prince of Deva
*VITALINUS of Glevum, the VOR-TIGERNUS
*VORTIMER, second son of Vitalinus
Uthir [Uther Pendragon], brother of Ambrosius
    Jordanus
    Ulfinus   warriors in service to Uthir

✝

PLACES

Abus Fluvius—R. Humber
Alba—Scotland
Altacluta—Dumbarton Rock
Ambrosiacum—Amesbury

the Barrow on the Ridgeway—Wayland's Smithy
Bannhedos—Castle Dore, Cornwall
Bremetennacum—Ribchester, in Lancashire
Britannia—the island of Great Britain
Calleva—Silchester
Camulodunum—Colchester
Cantium—Kent
Cluta Fluvius—R. Clyde
Cornovia—Cornwall
Dalriada—northern Ireland
Demetia—modern Pembrokeshire
Deva—Chester
Dubris—Dover
Dumnonia—the Cornish peninsula
Dun Ambros—Dynas Emrys, Wales
Dun Breatann—fortress of Dumbarton
Dun Eidyn—Edinborough
Dun Tagell/Durocornovium—Tintagel
Durobrivae—Water Newton
Durolipons—Cambridge
Durovernum Cantiacorum—Canterbury
Durnovaria—Dorchester, Dorset
Eburacum—York
Eriu—Ireland
the Fawwyth—the Fowey river, Cornwall
Gallia—France
Giant's Dance—Stonehenge
Glevum—Gloucester
Guenet—Gwynedd, North Wales
Hibernia, Eriu—Ireland
Isle of Glass or Isle of Apples—Glastonbury, Somerset
Isle of the Dead—Bardsey Isle, Wales
Isle of Maidens—Derwent Water, Lake Country
Isca Dumnoniorum—Exeter
Isca Silurum—Caerleon
Lindum—Lincoln
Londinium—London

Luguvalium—Carlisle
Madoc's Bay—Tremadoc Bay, Wales
Maridunum—Carmarthen
Mona—the Isle of Anglesey
Novantae lands—Dumfriesshire & Galloway
Noviomagus—Chichester
Portus Adurni—Portchester (Portsmouth)
Regnum—Chichester
Rithergabail—Episford, Kent
Rutupiae—Richborough, Kent
Sabrina Fluvia—the Severn River and estuary
Salmaes—the Solway
Sorviodunum—Old Sarum (Salisbury)
Stratcluta—Strathclyde
Tamesis Fluvius—Thames River
Tanatus Insula—Isle of Thanet, Kent
Tava Fluvius—the Tay
Treonte, Trisantona—the Trent
Vecta Insula—Isle of Wight
Venta—later Gwent, modern Monmouthshire
Votadini lands—southeast Scotland, from the firth of Forth to
    the Wall
Venta Belgarum—Winchester
Venta Icenorum—Caistor, Norfolk
Venta Silurum—Caerwent
Verulamium—St. Albans
the Wae—the River Wye
the White Horse—White Horse on Uffington Downs

THE WODAN'S CHILDREN TRILOGY

A retelling of the Siefried legend
with all the romance, magic, and myth richly
detailed and skillfully unveiled

By DIANA L. PAXSON

THE LORD OF THE HORSES
76528-4/$5.99 US/$7.99 Can

DRAGONS OF THE RHINE
76527-6/$5.99 US/$7.99 Can

THE WOLF AND THE RAVEN
76526-8/$5.99 US/$7.99 Can